THE COWBOY'S FORBIDDEN BRIDE

TAYLA ALEXANDRA

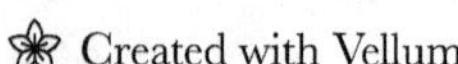 Created with Vellum

DEDICATION

Thank you to the One who gives His grace freely.

ALSO BY TAYLA ALEXANDRA

All Titles by Tayla Alexandra

Her Sweet Billionaire Romance Series

Her Billionaire Dream

Her Billionaire Jackpot

Her Billionaire Wish

Her Billionaire Chauffeur

Her Billionaire Scoundrel

To Trust Again - A novella

Finding Trust Series

Finding Alissa

Loving Josie

Reclaiming Bailey

Chasing Kennedy

A Billionaire's Tale Romance Series

The Billionaire Recluse

The Cinderella Ball

Bucket list Billionaire Multi-author Series

Beached with a Billionaire

* * *

Blushing Brides Series
The Billionaire's London Bride
The Cowboy's Forbidden Bride

❧

The Falling Series
The Act of Falling
The Law of Falling

❧

The Billionaire's UnWelcome Home

GET TAYLA ALEXANDRA'S STARTER LIBRARY FOR FREE

Sign up for my no spam newsletter and get the novella – *To Trust Again*, the Christmas short *Wrapped in Love*, and Brother of the Bride (Companion to The Cowboy's Forbidden Bride) and lots more exclusive content, all for free.

Details can be found at the end of the book.

1

______

EZRA

Ezra McCain headed for the front door. "I'm not doing it. No way. I'm done." Opening the door, he rushed out, slamming it tightly behind him. If he were lucky, it would give him a few extra seconds to get away. He stumbled down the porch steps and out into the open expanse of desert, searching for a place to run. Hide.

Blinding heat assaulted him as the blazing sun beat down on his body. Sweat beaded instantly on his forehead, and his eyes dotted from the brightness. Finding nowhere to hide, he took off away from the house.

Before he was only a few yards away, the door swung open, hitting the side of the house with a thud.

"Ezra, you get back here," the old man called. "You're a part of this whether you like it or not."

"I'm not going to do it. This is not the same. People are going to get hurt." Ezra picked up his pace.

Work boots hit the ground right behind him.

Garret was an old man, but he was tough. For as long as Ezra knew him, no one had ever backed out on him. If they had, they'd been met with a bullet right between the eyes. To be fair, he'd never seen it happen. He'd soon find out.

"Come back here, Ezra! Let's just talk about it."

"There's nothing to say." His hands shook so badly, he balled them into fists. "You may be a killer, but I'm not. You'll have to shoot me in the back, old man." Ezra picked up his pace to a jog.

There was no way he was getting out of the situation alive, but he'd rather be dead than do another dirty job for Garrett Malone.

"I raised you!" Garrett called, his voice cracking. "When you were on the streets, with nowhere to go, I took you in!"

Ezra stopped in his tracks, his heart thumping wildly. Dust settled heavily on his boots. The steps behind him halted at the same time. Refusing to turn and meet the barrel of Garrett's pistol, he waited. The raspy breath, well within his hearing, told him Garrett was close enough to blow his head off in an instant. But that's not what halted his retreat.

It was the truth of Garrett's words that had sliced through him like a blunt knife. Since he'd been a young boy, Garrett had taken care of him. He'd fed him, clothed him, taught him to read and write, and he'd never once laid a hand on him as his own father had. But along with that came heavy manipulation. Ezra had been indebted to Garrett. He owed him his life. At that moment, Ezra was sure Garrett would take it. Boldly, he turned around to face the man who stood less than a yard away.

"I can't do it, Garrett. Petty theft is one thing, but this, what you're talking about, will get people hurt. I didn't sign up for that."

"Come back inside, boy." Garrett placed his hand on the butt of his gun holstered to his waist. "Let's just talk about this."

"There's no more talking, Garrett. Either shoot me now or let me go."

Garrett watched him closely, his hand never leaving his gun.

"Go on then." Garrett nodded grimly. "Go on and leave."

Ezra stayed firmly planted in his place. The wind kicked up dust as a tumbleweed skittered between them. Ezra kept his focus on the man's face as sweat dripped down his forehead, burning his eyes. Still, he didn't blink.

The fear of being shot in the head was something, he realized in that instance, that he didn't want to experience. There had to be more to life than dying as a common thief at twenty-five.

"Go on. I won't shoot you." Garrett nodded again. "You're like a son to me."

Garrett's grip on the butt of his gun was so tight, his knuckles turned a brilliant white. His hand quaked, shaking the weapon beneath.

Ezra knew that, despite the tremor, Garrett would get off a clean shot to the head without a problem. He searched the cold, unflinching eyes of his opponent, but found nothing there. Not even a small flicker of whether he planned to shoot him or let him go.

On the off chance he was telling the truth, Ezra turned and sprinted off.

The sound of gunshots hit his ears just as bullets came flying his way. He picked up his speed and headed west. Not that any direction was a safe choice, he'd just been that way many times before and was familiar with the lay of the land.

Garrett let out a loud howl as if he was sport-hunting coyotes. There was nowhere to hide in the barren land. The desert brush was widely spread, leaving no hope for cover.

Another shot rang out, hitting Ezra in the shoulder. Pain flared through his body as if he'd run straight into a blazing fire, but he didn't stop. He couldn't stop. He was a far enough distance away that Garrett would not get another bullet into his body, but if he slowed down, Garrett would come after him. And the next shot would be straight to the head.

Dizziness overcame him as Garrett laughed off in the distance. "Better keep your mouth shut, boy!" he called. "Next shot'll be right between the eyes."

There was no chance of Ezra ever revealing anything about the crimes Garrett had committed. Ezra was an accomplice, and he'd rot in prison right alongside him if he spoke a single word against him. That was a fact that had been drilled into him each time they committed another felony.

"We're in this together, boy. I go down, you go down."

Blood soaked his shirt. His head spun out of control. The world around him became a low hanging cloud in front of his eyes. Nausea kicked in as saliva filled his mouth. No longer able to go an inch more, he fell to his knees, spewing the remnants of his last meal out over the desert floor. With each wretch of his body, his shoulder screamed in unbearable pain.

God, help me!

Ezra stumbled to his feet and stumbled only a few more paces before he could go no more. Falling to the ground, he emptied the rest of his stomach contents and fell face down into vomit.

Darkness surrounded him.

His sorry life passed before his eyes.

A scrubby little boy, sitting on the street curb, crying for the mother he could no longer remember and a father who didn't love him. Dirty tears streaked down his face. He held a half-eaten, bruised Granny Smith in one hand and the seven cents he'd found on the street in the other. His dark black, scraggly hair hung loosely in his face. Wiping snot on his smelly t-shirt, he looked up to the sky, asking for help from the great unknown.

The scene skipped to a father in a drunken stupor, a belt held high as he beat that same small boy.

His drunken father screamed obscenities at him. Berating him with each painful stripe. The child sat crunched into a ball, unable to lift his head for fear he would anger his father more. But the pain, it had ceased after the first few hits, his body and soul, numb to the world.

Late in the night, his father snored loudly on the couch, the belt still hanging from his hand, a brown bottle in the other. Creeping quietly past, he ran for the kitchen and stole every cent of the beer money from his father's jar. A crash sounded. He shrunk in fear. Waiting for the wrath to come. It didn't.

He tiptoed past the beast. The bottle lay on the floor below, clear liquid puddling on the tile. In the dead of summer, he ran hard and far. He didn't stop until he reached the old-west city of Tombstone.

"I'll never go back," he cried out to the city that didn't hear him. "You'll never hit me again."

Skipping backward as though sucked through a wormhole, Ezra was sitting at his mother's bedside.

She touched his hand. "Don't let this create bitterness in your heart, Ezra. I'll be watching from heaven."

His brain settled back on the streets of Tombstone.

Same dirty boy, eating food the tourists had left in an overfilled trash bin. The western street show was reenacting the shoot-out at the O.K. Corral. He grabbed his imaginary gun from his hip, pretending he was Wyatt Earp.

Pow! Pow!

Outlaw Billy Clanton lay dead in the street.

An old man sidled over to him. He'd looked like Wyatt Earp himself with his worn-out jeans, a western shirt, a gun holstered to his waist, and a cowboy hat clopped to his head. Only the cowboy had no badge.

"How about a hot meal, boy?"

Hungry, dirty, and completely broken, the boy holstered his imaginary gun and left with the stranger.

The ten-year-old watched in awe as the streets of Tombstone led out into the countryside, where not a vehicle could be seen for miles around. Chewing on his burger greedily, his fear of the cowboy had been less than the brutal abuse he'd already suffered.

The car stopped at a small farm with nothing but desert as far as the eye could see. The Wyatt Earp look-alike cleaned the boy up and nursed him back to health.

He was that broken boy, and he owed a lot to that man. He'd done everything the cowboy had told him to do. And now, as the angels from Heaven surrounded him, it was time to meet his maker.

But the angelic beings spoke to him — *Not yet, Ezra. It's not your time.*

The scorching sun burned down on his neck as his eyes opened. Lying face down in a puddle of his own vomit, he lifted his head. Not sure if he was dead or alive, Ezra leaned up to get a look. If he was in hell, it sure looked a lot like the desert.

His lips were cracked, his mouth tasting of a dead skunk. How long had he been lying there? A day, a week, only a couple of hours? Either way, he'd need to get out of the sun before it sucked up every ounce of water inside of him.

Willing himself to move through the blinding pain and blazing heat, Ezra used his good arm to creep along the ground like an injured Gila Monster, stopping with each movement to endure the pain. After what seemed like hours, he'd slid himself over to a bush that lent him only the smallest amount of shade.

Thoroughly beat, he closed his eyes against the sweat drenching his face and begged for the angels to come and take him back. Only, maybe that wasn't such a good idea. Certainly, his soul had been damned to a burning lake of fire. He'd done sold it to the devil. It was too late to call on God.

After some time, he gained a bit more strength. But it was all for naught. The sun was setting along the mountains, creating a glorious array of purples and reds. Soon, the coyotes would smell the fresh aroma of blood. Piece by piece, they would eat him alive.

Too tired to care anymore, he laid his head in the shade and hoped death would come soon, if only to rid him from his blinding pain.

As the sun declined, a rattle shook in warning as a horse galloped up from behind. His fate was near. He'd either take a shot in the head or die the slow death of rattlesnake venom. Either way, Ezra closed his eyes and prayed for God to forgive him of his sins.

As the shot rang out, the world went black.

2

―――――――――

CHARLOTTE

"Where is that boy?" The sun had set over an hour before, and her brother Cole had still not returned. "It doesn't take half a day to sell one horse."

Charlotte Spencer ran a soft brush over Clementine, their pregnant mare. Soon she would deliver, and once the foal was weaned, they'd have another mouth to feed. Tears came to her eyes as she wondered how they would ever manage.

Taking a glance out the stable door, she saw nothing but the faint outline of the ranch-style home her father had built before she was born. Not even the motion-sensor floodlight that hung over the porch illuminating the drive had cut on signaling he was back.

Watch over him, please.

Turning back, she glanced at the vast barrenness of the stables. It saddened her. At one time, every stall was full, and now they were down to a handful of horses. What was once a high functioning farm was down to a few chickens and one milking cow who was almost past her time of producing.

She'd trusted God with her very being, but the work was just too much. At one time, she'd had enough faith to move mountains, but lately, it was waning so much, she could barely kick over an anthill.

7

"You've got to help us soon. We can't do it by ourselves."

The ranch had been passed down to them by their father, and since her parents' death, it had dwindled away to nothing more than a riding stable. What had once been acres of vast land, with thousands of horses, was now a few acres with only ten horses and one on the way. Nine if Cole was able to sell.

The clomp of hooves in the distance alerted her that her younger brother had finally made it back. She just hoped he sold Sapphire and brought them enough money to get through the summer lull.

It was all they could do to turn the place into a riding stable that, at peak season, brought them in the money they needed to live off of. Only each year, the money was stretching less and less, and the expenses mounted on top of each other.

Charlotte went to the stable door. The floodlight kicked on as Cole came into view. She waited for the dust to settle, then met her nineteen-year-old brother riding up on Samson, their oldest, most reliable Morgan. With a sigh of relief that he wasn't leading the Appaloosa mare behind him, she ran toward him.

"How much did you get for her?" she called, hoping it would be enough to get them through the month. But as soon as Cole came fully into the light, she realized something was wrong. "What happened? Why is your shirt off? Cole, it's got to be a hundred and twenty out here."

The bright light above shone down like a spotlight, revealing his shoulders were an angry red. It was going to blister. As he stared at Charlotte, unspeaking, his haunted eyes were scaring her. She glanced down to see blood smeared on his hands and arms. Yet he didn't look hurt.

"Why aren't you answering me? Where's your shirt? Where did all that blood come from?" Thinking he must have shot a rabbit or a deer, she glanced behind him. That's when she caught sight of the bulk of a man that was strapped to the back of Cole's horse.

Her hand went to her mouth. Had Cole shot someone on accident? He was a perfect shot. That was an impossibility.

Cole jumped down, untied the ropes that held the man to the

horse, and gently pulled the lifeless body after him. Guiding him with his forearms, his muscles strained at the weight of the grown man. Taking quick strides, she marched closer to him.

"He's been shot." Cole raised his blood-tainted hands. "I patched him up as best as I could, but he's not going to make it if we don't get him to the hospital."

Charlotte kept a safe distance between her and the lifeless body, as she inspected the bloody man lying flat on the ground. All she could think of was that something was not right about the situation.

"You can't… he… what happened?"

"You wanna help me here?"

"How did you get him on top of Samson?" Cole was strong, but the bulk of a man had to be at least twice his size. Much too big for him to maneuver up that high.

"Come on, sis. Help me out here. I'll tell you all about it when we get him into the back of the truck."

Cole wrapped his arms around the underarms of the unconscious man and clasped his hands together across the broad chest. Charlotte watched, too stunned to move. There was so much blood all over his chest and shoulders. Charlotte wasn't necessarily squeamish around blood. There was just so much. And if Cole hadn't shot him, who had?

"Uh, sometime today?"

"What if he's dead?" she whispered.

"He will be if you don't help me. Grab his legs."

With an icy shiver, she placed her arms over the top of his legs, grabbed from the bottom of his dirty jeans and heaved him up around his ankles. Together they half-dragged, half-pulled him to their old, rusty truck.

"Stop." Charlotte sucked in a deep breath, wiping the sweat that cascaded down her face with her shoulder sleeve. "Just give me a second to breathe."

He was brawny. His limp muscles showed that he'd done many a day of hard labor. His shoulder-length black hair was crisp with blood and other undetermined fluids. Cole's shirt was wrapped haphazardly around his broad shoulder in a makeshift bandage. Blood seeped through, soaking it a bright crimson.

"Let's bring him inside."

Cole looked at her, confusion in his eyes. "I thought we were going to get him in the truck. We have to take him to the hospital. He'll die if we don't."

"Hospital's three hours away. He won't make it. Call Doc Evans."

"Doc Evans? Can he work on humans?"

"Can't be much different from horses. Let's get him inside and let him take a look. He can decide what to do next."

Cole nodded, wiped the sweat from his brow, and they carried the wounded man to the porch. Charlotte set his legs gently onto the hardwood flooring and opened the door. Cole struggled inside with the weight of the guy pushing his forearms to the limit. Charlotte took in another deep breath as she watched the lifeless feet drag across the living room floor. Inside, she grabbed the throw blanket from the back of the couch and draped it over the cushions. Not that it would do much good. The blood would soak through.

"Let's lay him down here, and call Doc."

Together, they hefted him one more time. Charlotte's muscles stung as she lifted his legs as high as she could to get him onto the couch.

"He's going to ask. What do I say?" Cole asked, breathing as heavily as she was.

"Tell 'em the truth. He'll come."

Cole shook his head and pulled his cell phone from his pocket. "This is going to be an interesting conversation." He went out to the porch to make the call. Once Cole was outside, Charlotte watched the man. What had she gotten herself into? She should have just allowed Cole to take him to the hospital in the truck. It wasn't her responsibility whether the man lived or died, but something inside her urged her to bring him into the house.

Lifting his wrist, she checked his pulse. He was alive. The slow, steady rise of his chest told her he was breathing as well. The dried blood on his shirt was a good sign that the bleeding had stopped. Or at least slowed considerably.

Charlotte headed for the kitchen to grab a bottle of water. She was parched, and he was certainly not going anywhere in his condition. Drinking down the entire bottle, much too fast, she wiped the sweat dripping from her forehead then went back to the couch where the stranger lay motionless.

He was completely unconscious. The blood that soaked his upper body and stuck his shirt to his chest was more than Charlotte had ever seen on any other human being.

The rancid odor of vomit wafted up to her nostrils, making her gag. She stood, went back to the kitchen, and grabbed a rag from the drawer. Filling a pot with warm, soapy water, she carried it back to the couch and wiped his chiseled cheeks and neck. Stroking the stiff hair that clung to his neck, the rag came back a dark crusted mess. She rinsed the cloth again and ran it back through his hair, pulling it gently from where it stuck to his neck.

There was nothing she could do about the smell emitting from his shirt until the doctor got there and examined him. There was no way she would take off the makeshift bandage Cole had tied around his shoulder. Pulling it off could start the bleeding all over again.

Wrinkling her nose, she rinsed the rag out again and placed it over the offending odor. It was the best she could do.

Cole came back into the house and stood over the couch. "He's on his way."

"What happened? Where did you find him?"

"He was out in the brush just east of here. I thought he was dead. I was just about to call the police when he moved. There was a rattlesnake in the brush, and his rattle was shaking. I knew it was just about to strike him, so I shot it's head off. He's tied to the back of the horse."

"East of here?" Charlotte asked as the information gave new meaning to her. "By Mr. Monroe's place?"

"Only about a half a mile away. Maybe less. Think he came from there?"

The image of a dark-haired, tall teenage boy caught in her

head. She looked back to the stranger. Was it him? She'd only been thirteen the one and only time she'd laid eyes on him. They'd met before. Only briefly, but they had met.

Her father's coarse words rang in her head. *Charlotte Renee, you stay away from that boy. He's up to no good.*

She'd never seen him again, but she dreamed about him from that day on. As much as her father wanted to protect her, Charlotte couldn't help wondering what the young boy was doing living with the irritable man whose small farm never produced much of anything. Mr. Malone drove the finest of cars, wore expensive clothing, yet lived in a run-down shack of a home. Something hadn't been right about him. Her father had been right in protecting her.

Could it be him?

She touched his face. His bristly, weatherworn skin reminded her of a younger version of her father. Hard working and strong, yet he'd been so caring. She missed the days when he wrapped his arms around her, tickling her until she screamed. He taught her how to ride a horse, to care for them, to love them.

Treat them with care, and you'll have a friend for life, Charlie girl.

The edges of her eyes burned with unshed tears for all she'd lost.

A vehicle pulled into the dirt driveway, setting off the outside light. Charlotte ripped herself away from the memory and stood.

She turned to Cole. "See if that's Doc."

Cole stared at her for a moment, confusion in his eyes at her display of emotion. She nodded for him to go. Without another word, he turned and went to the door.

Moments later, Doc Evans followed Cole in and came sidling up next to her. He was wearing his usual tan Stetson, black, button-down shirt with a horseshoe bolo tie, blue jeans, and carrying a black bag at his side. "What do we got here?"

"He's been shot." Charlotte's face flushed. "I'm afraid if we don't get him checked out, he won't make it to the hospital."

"I'm not exactly a people doctor," Doc Evans rubbed his chin thoughtfully. "But I've bandaged up a man or two. Let me take a look."

Charlotte moved to the back of the couch as another memory strolled through her brain.

"Name's Ezra." *The boy grinned as he tipped his way-too-big cowboy hat.* *"What's your name?"*

Completely enthralled in the boy's warm brown eyes, broad shoulders, and silly grin, she whispered back, "Charlotte."

"You live around here?"

"Just past those trees." She nodded toward her home. "You live here, too?"

"Yup. Over there." He pointed in the direction of Mr. Monroe's house.

"Charlotte Renee!" her father called. "You get back over here. You have no business with that boy."

"See ya around." He waved shyly.

"See ya."

Something about the boy had moved her young heart that day she'd met him so long ago.

Ezra. She remembered his name as if he'd said it only moments before.

Forcing herself back to reality, she watched as Doc Evans snapped on a pair of latex gloves, gently pulled the knot from Cole's crimson-stained shirt, and lifted it from around his shoulder. Next, he cut the bloody shirt right up the middle, exposing his bare chest. Pushing it to the side, he inspected the wound. "Came in through the back and made a clear exit here." He pointed to the clotted wound. "Bleeding has stopped. You did a good job of wrapping it," he said to Cole, who beamed with pride.

"By the looks of it, he's lost a lot of blood." He examined the wound closer. "Looks like a clean shot straight through. I suggest you get him to the hospital as soon as he's able, though. He's going to need a good dose of antibiotics and painkillers. In the meantime, keep his wound elevated and clean. I'll get him stitched up really quick." He dabbed at the wound with gauze, placed several unopened ones on the coffee table. "I'll leave these here for you." He then pulled out what looked like a roll of fishing line and a needle from his bag and closed the wound. "Help me lean him on his side," he said to Cole.

Cole leaned him forward, and the vet stitched the entrance

wound. He placed a large square bandage over the top of each wound and taped it down.

"Okay. That's the best I can do." He stood, pulling the gloves from his hands, and folded them inside of each other. "The rest'll be up to the hospital."

Charlotte nodded, staring at the bloody man lying on her couch. She got the feeling that taking him to the hospital might raise more questions than she knew how to deal with. Rumor was, Mr. Monroe had brought him into his home as a young child and made to do his bidding. What kind of investigation would be conducted into something like that? Surely the police would be called for a gunshot wound.

She'd asked about him once after overhearing a conversation her parents were having over their suspicions. She was sent to her room for eavesdropping and never brought up the topic again.

Her father was a firm but fair man and had always kept her best interests at heart. Her mother, the obedient wife, never went against her father's wishes. That was just the way it had always been. Right up until her father died, and she'd had no choice but to drop out of her first semester of veterinary school to help her mother on the ranch.

"I wouldn't want to give him anything I have on hand. Horse tranquilizers will put him out good, and might just kill him." He chuckled. "Once he wakes, give him over-the-counter painkillers until the hospital can prescribe something stronger. Keep his bandage clean, and watch for any sign of infection. He'll be up and around in a couple of days." The doctor stood to leave, but then swiveled on his heels to face her. "The hospital is going to want to know how he got shot. If he's who I think he is, you might want to have a good story for this one."

Charlotte already knew that. Unless it was some kind of hunting accident, and she doubted it was, someone had it out for him. He might not last a day in the hospital before his life was snuffed out. A chill ran through her clear to her bones.

"What if we don't take him?"

"It's my full recommendation that he be seen by the hospital, but I understand the position this puts you in." He glanced down at Ezra. "And him." His eyes showed deep concern.

"I think we'll take our chances."

She had no idea how she'd explain if he died on her couch, either. She was taking a huge chance by not following the law and reporting it. Something told her he had a better chance of survival there in her house than anywhere else.

He nodded solemnly. "I'll see what I can do about antibiotics to help him fight infection, and some stronger painkillers. Oh and keep the wound elevated as best as you can."

"Thanks, Doc," Cole said. It was obvious he didn't know what was going on in their heads. He'd only been a toddler at the time Ezra had mysteriously shown up at the Monroe house, and no one had mentioned him much since.

As soon as the doctor left, he asked, "Why aren't we taking him to the hospital?"

"I'm not sure yet. Let's talk to him when he wakes. If he is who I think he is, and even if he's not, the police are going to want to know how he got shot and how we came to find him."

"I'll tell them the truth. I found him lying half-dead in the brush. I got the snake to prove it."

It wasn't every day a person found a man dying in the desert, and Cole was overzealous about his heroism. Charlotte knew better, though. Whatever had happened was the work of Garrett Malone. If he found out his shot had not been fatal, trouble would surely follow. She was not wrong about it. Even without seeing his warm brown eyes, deep down in her soul, she knew the stranger was the same boy she'd met long ago. He had to be.

Charlotte said a word in prayer over him, asking God to heal his wound.

She'd been asking for help on her ranch ever since her father had passed away, and her mother shortly after. Could God have sent help in the form of the mysterious boy who had haunted her dreams? The boy who was now as clearly a man as she was a woman?

"Charlie?"

At the sound of her nickname, Charlotte realized she'd been staring at the man the entire time. "Get him one of Dad's shirts."

Without question, Cole headed from the room. Usually, her brother put up a fuss about being told what to do by his older sister, but after seeing a man almost die, she figured he was a little too shook up for back-talk.

Gently, she cut Ezra's tee-shirt up each arm sleeve and to the collar. She stood as it flopped down onto the couch. Heading back into the kitchen, she filled the pan with fresh water, and brought that, along with a clean rag, back to the couch and washed his chest gently, avoiding the wounded area.

Questions rolled through her head. What had happened to him? Had Garrett Malone finally lost his marbles and went off the deep end? Rinsing the rag, she set about one more time cleansing his chest, neck, and face with warm water. He smelled almost human again. She just had to get that shirt out from under him and out of the house.

Looking down to his faded blue jeans, she saw they were dirty, but not much of the vomit had gotten on them. She was thankful for that. There was no way she wanted to be wiping down his private parts. The thought alone made her face heat.

Cole came back with one of their father's t-shirts and handed it over to her. "Help me get him up just enough to pull the old shirt from under him."

Cole shifted on his feet. "Are you sure we should do that?"

"I don't know, but that smell is taking over the house, and Doc Evans said to keep him clean. This must qualify, right?"

"I guess so. I still think… Charlie, what if he dies right here on our couch? What are we going to do? Bury him in the backyard?"

She didn't want to think about that happening. "Just lift him gently, and I'll pull the shirt out."

Cole shook his head, placed his hands on Ezra's bareback, and pushed as Charlotte pulled the shirt from underneath him and tossed it into the water pan.

A moan broke out, startling them both. Cole let go and jumped back. Ezra's head bobbed slightly, and he opened his eyes. He grabbed for his head instantly, but not before his eyes met hers. Charlotte's throat constricted. It was him. She hadn't doubted it from the moment she'd seen him, but the eyes, they confirmed it.

"Have I died and gone to heaven?" He shook his head slightly. "No. Too much pain to be heaven."

"Cole, grab the painkillers from the bathroom cabinet and get him a bottle of water."

Her brother rushed off to the kitchen.

The second he left, Charlotte regretted being alone with him. Not that she feared him, but maybe she should. A lot had transpired in the twelve years since she'd seen him last.

She'd heard the rumors about the old man, and none of them were good. In her heart of hearts, she wanted to believe that Ezra had no part of the underhanded business Mr. Monroe was conducting. But assuming that would be foolish. Charlotte was anything but. She'd learned hard and fast what it meant to protect her family. Still, she had compassion for him.

"Do you remember what happened to you?" she asked gently, wishing she could fall into those deep brown eyes and never return to the hardship she'd endured over the past couple of years.

3

____

EZRA

zra squinted against the fog that shadowed his brain. Gradually, he brought the face that stared at him with concern, creasing her brows into focus. His heart thudded in rhythm with the throbbing in his shoulder.

Without a word, he watched the woman sitting next to him on the edge of the couch. She was so close that if his pained body would allow him to move a muscle, he'd reach out and touch her sweet face.

He'd have recognized the girl anywhere. His first love. Charlotte. He'd been so enamored with the sweet beauty from the first moment he laid eyes on her. So much so that he'd run off to her ranch every chance he got to get a glimpse of the strawberry-blonde hair that always seemed a tousled mess. At fifteen, he'd wanted to run his fingers through it, to calm the wayward strands. Her thin body that had been just developing the curves of womanhood had intrigued him for days on end. And those deep green eyes were the stuff his dreams were made of.

He blinked several times to comprehend what had happened that led him to her home. Why he was lying stiffly on her couch. How he had ended up with her looking down at him. The last thing he remembered was being so weak, he couldn't move. That rattlesnake poised to strike, and a horse riding up from behind. Had she been the one who came upon him? He'd been so sure it was Garrett coming to finish him off. But that made no sense. Garret didn't own a horse.

He couldn't dare tell her who he was. He was a bad person, raised by an even worse man. His first instinct was to run as far away from her as he could. If he'd had an ounce of energy, he would. There was no way the situation would end up well. If Garret found out he was there, they would all be in danger.

"Ezra?"

The sound of his name rolling from her lips sent his head spinning. He closed his eyes. She knew who he was, and that in itself was a dangerous thing. He tried to move, but no part of his body was cooperating.

"Lie back. You've been shot. The doctor bandaged you up, but you're going to need a good round of antibiotics to keep an infection from starting."

"No doctors." His head swirled again, and he opened his eyes for a moment. But the pain was just too much to bear. He closed them again. "No doctors," he whispered. "Please."

"You've already been seen." Her words jumped around in his tired head. "The doctor said you should——"

"What doctor?" His eyes flicked open as the realization of what she was saying hit him like an anvil. Adrenaline pumped through his veins. His heart leaped with fear. Any moment the police would be there, and he would be arrested. Taken in for questioning at the very least.

"Doc Evans. He's a veterinarian, but he checked you out fully. He says, with some antibiotics and pain meds, you should be as good as new in no time."

"A veterinarian?" His fears were dissuaded for only a moment. Clutching the couch, he tried to pull himself up to a sitting position.

"Cole?" she called, her raised voice vibrating through his head. "We need that medicine."

"Coming," her brother called back. The sound of boots clacked on the hardwood floors. "Sorry. I didn't know if you wanted Ibuprofen or Tylenol. We have aspirin, too."

"Give me the Tylenol." She held out her hand. "We'll alternate that with the Ibuprofen."

Reaching out her hand, she helped him to a sitting position. The pain was so intense that he held his breath, trying not to scream out in agony. There was no way he was going to walk out of there on his own two feet. At least, not until he'd recovered some.

"Here." She held her hand out with a couple of small pills cradled inside.

With shaky fingers, he took them and popped them in his mouth. What he must look like to Charlotte all shot up and weak. Not exactly how he imagined they would meet again.

Cole handed him a bottle of water.

"Let's get that shirt on him so he can lie back down." Charlotte went around behind him, grabbed the clean shirt, and brought it gently over him until his head reached through the top. "Can you lean forward? Cole, steady him."

Cole went to the front, pulled the coffee table closer to the couch and sat on the edge. "Grab onto my arms for support."

Cole was only inches away. Still, it seemed a long way to bend his burning shoulder. Holding his breath again, he leaned forward. His shoulder screamed out in pain, but he refused to cry out in front of Charlotte.

As his back left the couch, Charlotte let out a gasp. The vivid sound of her sucking in her breath made him cringe inwardly as she pulled the shirt down over his back. Ezra leaned back as she came around the side. With shaky hands, she maneuvered his undamaged arm into the sleeve. Her face was as white as the clouds, her eyes just as stormy, her mouth clenched so tight her lips seemed to disappear.

He understood the reason for her shock, and it wasn't the bullet wound. She'd seen the many scars his father had left on his back. She didn't say a word, so neither did he.

"We'll leave the other arm inside," she croaked. "I don't think we'll be able to get it in the sleeve."

He wanted to reach out to her, let her know it was okay. That those wounds had healed long ago. But it was an awkward moment, and his groggy brain couldn't find the words.

Grabbing several throw pillows, she piled them up on the end of the couch. "Doc says to keep it elevated." Her voice cracked as she spoke. "The wound, I mean. He said to keep it above your heart."

Letting it go, Ezra cringed at the pain and turned his body to meet the pillows. He'd not felt so much agony since his father had created those scars with his leather belt. He'd long since been used to them, but it wasn't a pretty sight.

Suddenly, he felt exhausted. Like his body was taking over the function of his brain. He was so tired, he couldn't keep his eyes open another second.

"Get some rest. I'll make you some soup." Charlotte's words were like echoes through a long tunnel as his mind went to a safe-haven where pain did not exist.

"I better get the horse back to the stable," the other voice slurred.

Ezra willed the agony to subside as his body fell into a deep sleep.

"HERE'S THE PLAN. We head to Phoenix in Bart's car. It's the most easily disguisable. We steal a car from an old… well, let's just say, the dirtbag has it coming. He deserves a nice long prison stay. Anyway, once we're in Scottsdale, we take out the Wells Fargo on Indian School Road. It'll be an easy job. Rhett, you and Ezra will hold the customers at gunpoint. Me and Bart will get whatever cash they got up front. No use trying for the big stuff. There won't be enough time. We got five minutes tops, in and out."

"What about security?" Rhett asked, tipping his chair back as he flopped his feet on top of the old wooden table.

"I'll take care of them." Garrett placed a hand on his gun belt and looked slyly to Bart.

Bart nodded, touching his own gun.

"It'll be an easy job. Once we get the money, we'll drop the car back off with

Joe and jump into Bart's. By the time we're back, the cops will be investigating him while we are splitting the dough. He's a dealer, and they won't hesitate to bring him in. It's an easy job with——"

"Now wait a minute." Ezra stood. "You gonna kill a man over some petty cash up front?"

"Ain't no one said nothing about killing a man. We're just setting him up for a nice long ride to the pen."

"The security guard. You plan on taking him out, don't you? And what about the customers? How many of them are gonna die?"

"You gone soft on me, boy?"

"You never asked me to kill a man before. What if there are women in there? Children."

The others laughed as if Ezra was the crazy one.

"Ain't no one gotta die." Garrett grinned evilly. "If they do what they're told, they'll be fine."

"And the security guard? How you getting around him without killing him?"

"You just leave that up to me."

The sight of spilled blood entered Ezra's head. No way he was going through with it. He stood and backed his way to the door. "I'm not doing it. No way. I'm done."

A WARM HAND touched his arm, and Ezra flinched. He opened his heavy eyes. The most beautiful sight stood over him, wearing a light-blue top that set off the green in her eyes. Her hair was pulled back in a soft bun with a few wayward strands falling down into her face. As she leaned forward, one strap slid off her shoulder. Freckles dotted her tanned arms. Her smile made his sleepy heart skip a beat.

"How are you feeling?"

"Tired." His eyes were thick with exhaustion, it was all he could do to keep them open. "How long have I been asleep?"

"A couple of days, off and on. Doc came by with some stronger pain pills and antibiotics. You don't remember taking them?"

Ezra shook the grogginess from his head. "Not really."

"Well, I've got you to eat a couple of times. Even got you up to use the bathroom."

Ezra stared at her, wondering if any of that were really true. He remembered none of it. "Must have been some good stuff he gave me. Hope it wasn't a horse tranquilizer."

Charlotte gave him that sweet smile that had melted his heart many times before. Only she'd never known just how she'd climbed her way into his heart over the years. He made sure of that. Ezra was the worst kind of scoundrel. He'd done too many things to ever be loved by someone so sweet and pure. Yet, there he was, staring into her beautiful green eyes, wishing he could hold her.

"Nope. Just something strong enough to dull the pain. You talk in your sleep, you know."

Ezra's face burned with heat. Fearing embarrassment, yet wanting to know, he asked, "Yeah? What did I say?"

"It was all a bunch of jumbled words, but I did make out you calling for me a time or two. I thought you actually needed something, but when I came around the couch, you were fast asleep. You snore like a buzz saw."

He was right. He didn't want to know. "Probably wanting more of those good pain meds." He pulled himself to a sitting position, marveling at how little pain he felt. "Where's your brother?"

"Don't do too much. You're still not healed." She touched his hand, sending warmth throughout his body. "Cole's out leading a trail ride. We only have four riders today. The summers are always rough for business."

"A trail ride?"

"Yeah. When Daddy passed, we turned the place into a riding ranch. People, mostly tourists visiting Tombstone, come out to ride the horses. But with the high-heat, we've been low on visitors. Comes with the territory."

Ezra closed his eyes tight, clearing the drug-induced fog from his head before he spoke again. "I thank you for nursing me back to health, but I better be on my way."

Charlotte placed a hand on his good arm, sending another wave of heat through his body. "Like I said, you're not healed yet. You still have a week's worth of antibiotics, and as soon as those pain meds wear off, you're going to be in a lot of pain."

"I can't stay. It's not safe."

Charlotte gave him a long look. "Ezra, if you're in danger, we should call the police. They can——"

"No police." He stood to his feet so fast that his head whirled and he fell back down to the couch.

"You're in no condition to leave. Please stay a little while longer."

Unfortunately, she was right. There was no way he'd make it past the front door.

"A few days, then I have to go. But please, no police."

Charlotte nodded as if she understood much more than he was saying. What did she know about the life he'd grown up with?

"Okay. A few more days, but Doc Evans says it could take months for you to heal fully."

"I don't have months." His voice was harsh, and he willed himself to speak more calmly. "I… Charlotte, I can't put you or your brother in danger."

"What happened?"

His mouth twisted as he worked through the emotions. "I can't say right now, but every moment I stay, I'm putting you in jeopardy." He'd rather die painfully than put her in the way of Garrett Monroe. If he found out the no-account, do-gooding family, as he called them, had taken him in, he wouldn't hesitate to make trouble for them.

"Okay, then." She turned away. "I have some work to do. I'll be back shortly." She left and returned a few minutes later with a bowl of soup and a cup of coffee. "I take it you can feed yourself?"

He nodded.

By her clipped words and the set of her jaw, he could see she'd been upset by him not wanting to confide in her, but it was for the best. It wouldn't be long before Garrett realized he wasn't lying dead in the desert somewhere, and when he did, he would make sure he finished the job. He'd had never been a violent person in particular, but he wasn't one to leave a job undone, either.

Ezra had made himself unfinished business. It would have been better for all concerned if he had died out there. Garrett would come looking for the body, and when his blood trail ended with hoof tracks that led to Charlotte's home, there would be trouble.

Garrett wouldn't start trouble for them if Ezra wasn't there. He was good at covering his tracks and wouldn't do something that would place him under the scrutiny of the Sheriff's Department.

He watched as Charlotte strolled out the door, allowing it to close heavily behind her. Wanting to call her back, but having nothing of value to say, he let her go.

He watched out the picture window as she stood, one toned arm resting on her slight hips, the other waving out to someone he couldn't see. Leaning up to get a better look, he saw Cole leading a team of four horses back to the house. Each horse carried a passenger holding firmly to the saddle horn. It looked to him like a family. A father, mother, and two young, giggling girls.

How did Charlotte make enough money to support her brother, the animals, and pay the annual property tax and utilities? How did they manage the ranch alone? Ezra would give anything to help them in their struggle. But he was no freer to help than a runaway slave before The Civil War. He was a marked man, branded by Garrett Malone.

Closing his burning eyes again, he allowed sleep to take hold. It was no use trying to stay awake. His body needed rest if he was going to leave in three days.

4

———————

CHARLOTTE

Charlotte put on a smile and waved as Cole and his group came in from the trail and up the dusty drive. Still seething inside over Ezra's childish refusal to tell her what happened, she tried to push it back for the moment.

She understood his fear of the police getting involved. But the law was there to protect citizens from tyrants like Mr. Malone. She'd known he would refuse help, it was why she hadn't called them to begin with, but someone had to stop him before more people got hurt or killed. What bothered her more than that was Ezra's refusal to explain why he was shot in the first place. How could she help him if he wouldn't open up to her?

Never had she met a more stubborn man in her life. How could he tell her not to involve the police and yet advise her in the same conversation that his being there was putting them in danger?

She had a mind to call them, anyway. Whatever Ezra had done to anger Mr. Malone could be settled right then and there. He certainly wasn't above the law. If they called the sheriff, he'd have to be arrested. She was determined to speak to Ezra again. She had to make him understand. But first, she needed to help the riders down and assist Cole with getting the horses unsaddled and watered.

"Did everyone have a good time?" she asked.

"I did!" the younger girl exclaimed. "We saw a jackrabbit and a coyote."

"I think my bottom is numb." Mr. Thompson rubbed his backside and climbed stiffly off his horse. "I'm too old for this."

"If you all would like to follow me to the stable store, fresh-squeezed lemonade and complimentary cactus candy is waiting for you." She helped the young girls down, grabbing the reins of their horses.

"Cactus candy?" The older girl, Cassy, wrinkled her nose. "Is that good?"

"I think it is." Cole grabbed the reins to the other two horses as Mr. Thompson helped his wife down. "Charlotte makes the best cactus candy in town."

"I want to try it!" Sandy, the younger girl said. "Can we feed the chickens, too?"

"You certainly can." Charlotte smiled. "If it's okay with your parents, I'll let you help me collect some eggs, too."

"Sure," the mother answered, walking bow-legged. "I need to stretch my legs first."

"I'll get the horses cleaned up and watered." Cole took the reins from Charlotte. "You go ahead and take care of our guests."

Charlotte thanked her brother and headed back to the store her father had started building before he passed away. Her mother had wanted the place to be a small cafe and resort for the tourists to stay and visit.

Her father had never gotten the chance to complete it. Charlotte and her brother had turned the place into a small shop where people could relax after their ride and buy snacks and souvenirs.

She spent much of her available off time sewing memorabilia stuffed animals and cacti for their guests to buy. Each embroidered with the C&C Trails emblem proudly at the back or bottom.

Cole was good at whittling and had made many wooden keepsakes for the shop. He'd invested in a small branding iron with the same markings so guests could remember their stay.

Every now and then, he'd find a dead scorpion or a snake rattle to encase in resin as a cool paperweight. The shop was small, but they made a good deal off of it year-round.

She led them inside, welcoming them to sit at the small seating area with table legs made from dead Cholla. The holey cactus skeleton gave off an old-west feel that their customers often enjoyed.

"Make yourself at home. I'll be right back."

Charlotte left for the kitchen unit in the back that held a mini refrigerator, hot plate, and a small sink. Her vision had been to turn it into a proper kitchen where she could offer a variety of lunch menu items to her customers like her mother had wanted. But without the funding, it had been only a dream. She pulled the pitcher of lemonade and a small plate of cactus candy from the refrigerator and brought it out to the family.

"Here you go." She set the lemonade on the table. "Freshly squeezed from our very own lemon trees. And this——" She held out the plate. "As promised, is cactus candy. I make it from the cacti right here on the ranch."

"What kind of cactus do you make it from?" Sandy asked.

"Probably the big Saguaro's," Cassy said. "Bet you can make a lot of candy with those."

"Actually, you *can* eat the fruit of the Saguaro, but it doesn't taste very good." Charlotte puckered her lips into a sour face. "It's rather bitter."

"A barrel cactus?" the younger girl guessed.

"The fruit from a barrel cactus is quite edible. It tastes something like a tart kiwifruit. But no, the candy comes from the Prickly Pear. Did Cole point some of those out to you?"

"I remember." Sandy bounced in her chair. "It was the pancake looking ones, right?"

"Those are the ones."

Charlotte wanted to get back to Ezra before he tried to slip out the back door and injure himself further, but her livelihood depended on making a sale. There were only a few scheduled riders throughout the summer, and she counted on the little money they made to get them through the slow months.

The family finished their drinks, tried a bit of the candy, and then looked around the small store. After picking out a stuffed animal for each of the kids, a scorpion paperweight for the father and a package of more cactus candy, she rang them up. Happy with the sale, she placed the money in the old-fashioned register, walked them out, and locked up the store behind her.

The girls automatically ran in the direction of the chicken coops. Charlotte smiled.

"Guess we got some chickens to feed." They'd already been fed, but a couple of little girl handfuls wouldn't hurt.

"Ever eaten green eggs and ham?" she asked, chasing after the girls.

"Green eggs? Like Sam I Am?"

"Yep. Depending on the breed, chickens lay all different colored eggs."

"I've only had white ones," Cassy admitted. "Scrambled."

Charlotte let them each pull a handful of grain from the bag and spread it on the ground for the chickens to peck. She allowed them to grab a warm green egg and bring them back to their parents.

"Can we keep them?" they begged.

Charlotte glanced through the porch picture window to see Ezra still lying on the couch sound asleep.

Good at least he hasn't tried to run off.

"Oh, I don't think so. Why don't you bring it back to the nice lady?"

The girls frowned, their shoulders shrinking in disappointment.

"I don't mind. If it's okay with you."

The husband stepped up, folded an extra bill into her hand and thanked her. "We had a great time. Thanks for everything."

The woman stood next to her husband. "We'll be back next year. I can promise you that."

"Thank you. Your girls are adorable. I'd love to have you back."

The husband chuckled. "It'll be another year before I'm able to mount a horse again."

"Come on, old man. We have a long drive home."

Charlotte watched them climb into their vehicle and drive away. She waved goodbye and headed back to the stable to help Cole finish getting the horses washed and watered.

"How'd we do?" he asked as soon as she entered.

"After the trail ride and souvenirs, two hundred dollars. Not much, but it will get us through a couple of weeks." She remembered the bill the guy had shoved into her hand and pulled it from her pocket. She hadn't wanted to check how much it was in front of them. "Two twenty."

"A tip. Nice. Yeah, with the money I got for Sapphire, we should be okay for the summer."

She hated that she had to give up the mare. But it only made sense. They were barely squeezing by with the price to care for ten, and with Clementine being pregnant, it was the right thing to do.

"Did you put the money in the register?" she asked as she brushed the last horse down and led him to the water trough.

"Yes. But Charlie, we need to talk." Cole was the only one in the world who could use the nickname her father had given her.

"About what?" She knew what, but she'd let him get it out.

"That guy in the house. Ezra. What if he's a dangerous criminal? And why do I feel like you know him from somewhere?"

"And how do you expect I know him? Since mom passed away, I haven't had time to go anywhere or do anything."

It was painful that their nearest neighbor was a criminal. All of her life, she'd never had one friend. But it was how her parents had wanted it.

The world is a harsh place, her mother had told her. *We bought this land to protect you from the bad things that happen out there.*

Even after they'd sold much of the land, it had been mostly turned into acres and acres of cotton fields planted by industrial growers with big machines.

"You get that look whenever you're around him."

"What look? The same one you give Samantha every time she comes to ride?"

Cole's face reddened. "Yeah, that one."

"Do you guys still email each other? Haven't seen her for a couple weeks." It was the perfect time to change the topic back to him.

"Yeah. And we talk on the phone when we can. What would you say to her coming down to visit?"

"She comes all the time. Of course, I wouldn't have a problem with that."

"I mean, more than just the day. You know, come and stay for a week or so."

"Oh no, you don't. Dad would flip over in his grave if he found out I let you and a girl spend the week together unsupervised."

"How are we ever going to spend time together? It's not like she can stay somewhere in town. We'd spend all our time traveling. Besides, she could stay behind the store. Dad built those rooms for guests. We should start using them."

She'd thought about that often, but the rooms were unfinished. Electricity and plumbing had been wired to the five rooms, but they were was no furnishings. There was only the one community bathroom half-finished in the middle with the toilets still not hooked up, and floor tiles that had yet to be laid stacked up along the wall. Her father had been in the middle of finishing it when he'd gotten sick. Her mother would have loved the place to be used for what it was intended, but the funding was just not there.

"We don't have the money to furnish the rooms. And where do you expect guests to shower and use the restroom?"

"I'll finish the bathroom myself. Dad bought all the stuff. It won't cost an extra cent."

It was a great idea, but there were still so many obstacles. "And the rooms?"

Cole rubbed the back of his neck. "I don't know."

The idea settled with her. The extra income would mean survival and not having to sell off any more horses or land. "If we can find some furnishings for the rooms, maybe we could make it work."

"What if we get married?" Cole asked, still stuck on having Samantha come and stay.

Ignoring his question, her head spun with ideas. "What if we took the money we got for the horse and bought furnishings for the rooms? Do you think people would come?"

"And if they don't, we'll be eating coyote and jackrabbit for dinner. No thanks."

It never ceased to amaze her how quickly her brother could go from thinking an idea was great to entirely dismissing it.

"And Quail. Cole, this was your idea, and I think we can do this. We can furnish a couple rooms at a time. How much can it cost to get a bed and a dresser in there?"

Charlotte could see the wheels spinning in his head once again. "I could cut down a couple of trees to frame some mattresses. I'm getting good at that. And what about the old bunkhouse? Maybe we could use the dressers from in there."

Charlotte thought about the open-style building that once held many ranch hands. It hadn't been used since her father passed and they'd had to get rid of the hired help. "The mattresses will be of no use, and the frames are probably too small to do anything with. But the dressers can be sanded down and stained."

"You think they're too small?"

"No. I don't think so. How much dresser space does a person need for a night or two?"

"Okay, then. And what about the beds?"

"Authentic bed-frames made from Palo Verde trees. Cole, you think you could do it?"

"I'm going to look it up online. I'm sure I could make one or two."

"I could sew some western-style bedspreads. Just two rooms for now." For the first time, she felt things could be looking up. The mattresses would be the most expensive, but maybe it could work. "What about that old wagon out behind the stable? I bet we could use the wheels to make a frame, too. Maybe we could really do this."

"Okay. Cool. Now, back to Samantha?"

"Cole, you're a genius!" Charlotte said. "If we can get a couple of roomers in here, it would solve all of our problems."

She envisioned a pit in the back where they could light a fire in the winter. They could advertise the place in Tombstone, on the internet, and a couple of other area towns. It just might work.

"And Samantha?" he prodded.

"We'll see, but Cole, no marriage yet. Don't rush things."

Cole's fist pumped up through the air. "Yes!"

He understood that when Charlotte said — we'll see, it meant if it were at all possible, it would get done. Laughing at his enthusiasm, she finished watering the horses and headed back to the house. For the first time since her parents had passed, Charlotte felt as though they might just have a plan to keep them going through the summer months.

As they headed up the steps of the porch, a loud groan emerged from inside the house.

"Sounds like something dying in there," Cole said.

"It sure does." And there was only one person in the house. "Better go see what's going on."

"You handle it. I'm going to check out that old wagon to see if there's anything usable from it."

By the time she made it up the stairs, the groaning had increased in volume and caliber. Was Ezra dying in there? She picked up her pace and opened the door. When Charlotte made it inside, he was laying back on the couch, moaning and groaning like a dying mule. Immediately, she forgot she was angry with him and rushed to his side.

"What's wrong?" Checking the clock on the mantle, she realized it was time for his pain meds.

Ezra lifted his head and opened his eyes as if he hadn't even heard her come in. "I have to pee!"

"Are you serious? You can't make it to the bathroom by yourself?"

"No!" He grabbed his abdomen. "I tried several times, but I can't get off this darn couch."

Unable to form words through her laughter, Charlotte held out a hand to help him up.

"You think this is funny?" He gave her a weighty stare and then smiled. Taking her hand in his, he pulled himself up.

"I like you better after you've had your medication," she quipped. "You know where the bathroom is."

Ezra shuffled to the back of the house at a snail's pace, his knees popping as he went. Grabbing onto the wall for support, he pushed inside the bathroom and closed the door.

A knock came at the front door. Wondering who it could be, Charlotte peeked out the window. Doc Evan's old dusty station wagon was parked in the driveway.

"Hey, Doc," she said, opening the door. "Come on in."

"How's our patient doing?"

"He's in the bathroom. He should be out soon."

"Good. He's up and around. Gotta keep that circulation flowing, but we don't want him to overdo it." He looked away for a second. "Hey, since I got you alone, I wanted to ask if you ended up taking him to the hospital. I know it's a touchy subject and all, but you know, I could lose my license if they found out I treated him without reporting it."

Charlotte shifted. "He says no police. I think he's worried what might happen to him if he reports it."

"Did he tell you what happened?"

"He won't speak about it, but I have a feeling it was Mr. Monroe. We all know some shady business has been going on over there for years. It's a shame no one has been able to catch him in anything."

"We'll keep it under wraps for now, but I have a feeling this isn't going to end well."

"Thanks, Doc. I wouldn't want to get you into any trouble," she mumbled. "I just don't know what kind of suffering it will bring to him. Or us."

"I have your best interest in mind. I can't see him being much of a threat right now, but I worry about you out here alone with him."

Charlotte didn't see the concern, but it was the second time that day someone had mentioned it to her. She'd distracted Cole easily, but the topic would come up again.

"We're going to move him out to one of the rooms behind the store as soon as he's up and around on his own."

"I'd feel much better about that." His eyes creased downward as the bathroom door opened, and Ezra came out. "There he is now. How are you feeling?"

"Like I got shot through the shoulder. Why're my legs so wobbly?"

"Because you haven't been exercising them. I suggest you get up and around as much as you can stand it. Nothing strenuous, though. No lifting or running marathons any time soon."

"Sounds like a plan," Ezra answered. "As soon as I'm able, I'll be moving on."

Doc Evans nodded. "You'll heal up in no time. You're one lucky guy to be alive right now. That shoulder injury could have been much worse if it had hit a tendon. And if Cole hadn't come along when he did, you'd have been a tasty meal for the buzzards."

Charlotte swallowed the knot that hung in her throat. The image of Ezra lying out there, bleeding to death, was not one she wanted to see. Now, all he talked about was getting out of there as if she were the plague. She saw no way to convince him to stay.

Like it or not, Ezra was set on leaving, and there was nothing, short of ripping his stitches out and reopening the wound, that would stop him from going. Something told her it wasn't simple pride that made him want to leave. No, he thought by leaving, he was protecting her. Maybe he was right. If only she knew the full story.

Doc Evans checked Ezra's wounds, cleaned them, and replaced the bandages. He said his goodbyes and Charlotte showed him to the door. She went back to where Ezra sat, trying to open the bottle of painkillers with one hand, and watched for a while before speaking up.

"Want me to do that for you?"

He fiddled with it for a while longer, but finally gave in and handed her the bottle.

"What happened to your parents?" he asked as she gave him a painkiller and the bottle of water from the table.

Charlotte sat across from him in the chair. "My father passed first." It was painful to talk about, but if she opened up to him, maybe he would do the same. "He suffered a brain tumor. When the symptoms first started, it was just severe headaches. As time went on, the symptoms progressed to where he couldn't even stand without falling, his vision became blurred, and he seemed to become confused by the simplest things. He kept telling my mother it was nothing, but she wanted him to be seen by a doctor. It was the first time I ever remember my mother pressing an issue. He refused to go. One day he was working and almost got trampled by the horses. My mother finally won that day. But by the time she rushed him to the hospital, the cancer had progressed too far for them to save him."

Ezra gave her a sad smile. "That's rough. How old was he?"

"He was only forty-eight. He should have had so much more time left with us." She took a deep breath to stave off the tears that bit at her eyes. "If only he hadn't been so stubborn."

Ezra touched her leg, sending shivers through her body. "You don't have to tell me any more. I'm sorry, I upset you."

For reasons she didn't quite understand, she wanted to continue. She'd held it all in for so long that it was freeing to let it out. It was something Cole avoided talking about like the plague. If she brought it up, he would shut down.

"My mom, she passed away only a couple of years back. She tried so hard to keep the ranch going. She did everything she could. We worked night and day, Cole didn't even get to finish high school. One day, I came in from feeding the horses, and she was lying on the kitchen floor. The doctor said she'd had a heart attack." She let the tears flow freely. "I didn't even get to say goodbye. The next thing I know, Cole and I are selling off horses and land just to make ends meet. My father had taken out a loan for the new building, and pretty much everything we got was put in to pay it off. Life quickly became a struggle to survive."

"You've had a rough past couple of years." He held her eyes for a long time.

Charlotte nodded to his shoulder. "It looks like you've had quite the past yourself."

She wanted to know the questions that had run through her mind ever since the day they met, but she wouldn't pry. It would only push him away. The brutal scars on his back came to mind, and she rubbed at the goosebumps on her arms

"You look tired. You should get some rest."

5

———

EZRA

Another week and Ezra was up and around. He'd contemplated leaving so many times, but after spending so much time with Charlotte and watching them struggle, he couldn't bring himself to leave her. His feelings for her grew deeper than ever.

During their time together, they'd shared moments he wouldn't give away for the world. There'd been so many times of closeness where they talked for hours, held hands, and shared their dreams with each other. He'd never felt so full in his life. No words of love were spoken, but they didn't need to be. He could feel deep within his heart that Charlotte Spencer was the only woman he'd ever wanted. She'd given him the will to live, and not only that, but to live rightly. Only one thing stood between them. That was his fear that each day he connected with her and loved her, was putting her life in more danger.

"Ready for our walk?" Charlotte held out her hand. "Doc's orders."

Walking with her at sunset had become the highlight of his day. Never before had he admired the glorious hues of the evening sky. And holding her hand as they strolled the banks of the San Pedro

River made him feel he could actually become an honest man. He could put away the past and start life anew. He'd never wanted a life of crime to begin with. The thought of becoming an honest cowboy and helping her on the ranch was all he ever wished for. But that wish could be dangerous.

Ezra took her offered hand and together they went outside. Even after all the time they'd spent together, her touch still did things to his heart that his brain refused to comprehend.

"I'm glad you decided to stay longer," she said, squeezing his hand.

"Me too." He turned to her with some effort. "You know I can't stay forever, though."

"About that. I think I may have some good news for you."

Nothing short of Garrett being buried six feet under would be enough to allow him to stay with her. "Oh, yeah. What's that?"

"On his way back from the feed store, Cole saw the sheriff at the Monroe house. He said Mr. Monroe was handcuffed and being loaded into the back of a county vehicle."

Ezra stopped in his tracks and faced her. That was some news he could work with. Had they tried to pull off that bank job? "Was anyone else arrested?"

Charlotte looked at him strangely. "Well, Cole didn't say, but I'm sure he'd have mentioned it if there had been more people there."

Leaning in, Ezra kissed her lightly on the cheek. "Thank you. That is good news.

Her face flushed, and she turned away.

"I like you, Charlotte Renee. Always have."

"I like you, too." Her head turned back to him in question. "Wait, how do you know my middle name?"

"From that first day we met. Remember? Your father saw us talking. He called for you to get away from me as if I was some kind of leper." He chuckled at the memory. The look on Charlotte's face when her father had called out to her was the same one she got when he kissed her cheek. The one that made him fall in love with her.

"You could've been any boy, and he'd have done the same. It was nothing against you, personally."

"Yeah, I get it." Maybe she believed that, but her father was protecting her from a thief. He didn't blame him. "That day, I fell in love with your soft curls, your sweet smile, and the way your cheeks blushed when you looked at me." He touched her cheek. "I didn't want you to leave."

"And here we are. Together again."

Ezra fought the urge to pull her in his arms and kiss her. This time on her sweet lips. But he didn't have to hope for long because she turned to him, leaned up on her toes, and pecked him on the lips. Admiring her boldness, he pulled her closer and deepened the kiss. Her hand came to the back of his neck as he took in her warm lips.

When she pulled away, he touched her reddened face. "Please don't tell me you regret it because I don't."

"I want you to stay." Her eyes pleaded with him. "Whatever happened, we can figure it out. Please say you'll stay."

"I want to, Charlotte. More than anything." He kissed her again. "But I can't make any promises."

"It's settled then." She released his hand. "You'll stay." With a dash, she ran off toward the river.

"Wait! I said no promises!" He straggled after her, a hand to his wounded shoulder. His body had a long way to go, but his heart was vibrant.

She was almost to the riverbank when she glanced back. Out of breath, Ezra rolled onto the ground, holding his arm and groaning.

"Ezra!" She rushed back to his side and bent down over him. "Are you okay?"

Pulling her to the ground beside him, he leaned in and kissed her again.

"You tricked me, you big lug!" She slapped at his good arm.

"Can I have one more?"

"You don't have to trick me to get a kiss." She leaned up on her elbow beside him and placed her lips softly on his.

A hunger grew inside him, stronger than he'd ever felt before. A longing to be a good man. To belong somewhere. There, with Charlotte.

"A penny for your thoughts?" She touched his face.

"All the pennies in the world couldn't pay for the depth of my thoughts."

"How about an IOU? I'm good for it."

"Let's get out of this dirt and go sit by the river."

"And you'll tell me?"

He nodded.

They stood, and he put an arm around her waist. "I think I really hurt myself."

"That's what you get for crying wolf."

Ezra grinned. He'd give a thousand hurts to feel her lips on his again.

6

____

CHARLOTTE

As they sat on the bank of the river, Charlotte didn't know what she expected him to say. The affection they'd shared over the last week had been deeper than she'd ever imagined. And then he'd kissed her cheek, and she'd wanted more. Maybe her daddy would be ashamed of her for being so bold to kiss Ezra, but she hadn't let that stop her. It was beyond all reason for her to love him, but she did.

"How did you get your education?" he asked. "There are no schools out this way."

"Oh, no you don't, Ezra McCain. You promised me facts. Start talking."

Ezra grinned and took her hand. "I don't remember promising, but if you're sure you want to know, I'll tell you."

"I do."

"And you won't hate me when I'm done?"

"I could never hate you."

"Don't bet your chickens on that one."

"Tell me."

"What do you want to know?"

She wanted to know where he came from, how he ended up

with a dirty rat like Mr. Monroe, how he got those stripes on his back, where his real parents were… and so many more questions, but she settled for one. "How did you get shot?"

Ezra shifted. "You would go right in for the kill." He stopped as if in deep thought.

"Don't tell me some half-truth. Please. I'm a big girl."

"You're more than a girl, Charlotte. You're a beautiful woman."

"You're stalling again." Still, she reveled in his words.

"It's hard to start there. You'd have to hear the entire story to understand the end."

"I'm listening."

Ezra leaned in and sighed. "I was six when my mother passed away. My father took it really hard. At first, he bottled it all up inside, but then he turned to a real bottle. He drank himself to sleep most nights. From my bedroom, I listened to him sob. He was a shattered man, and I, too, was broken. I yearned for my mother's love." He sniffled.

"How did she die?"

"Dad said it was cancer. I'm not sure what kind. All I know is that she died a slow, agonizing death. And it killed my father and me." He stopped, picked up a rock, and threw it into the river.

Charlotte's heart broke for the young boy who had to endure such a loss. She knew loss, but she'd had a good childhood before enduring that hardship.

"So, by the time I was eight, my father had lost his job and did nothing but sit at home and drink. He took his anguish out on me. Over and over again. I was a constant reminder of my mother. By the time I was ten, I'd had enough. I ran away, and that's where I met Garrett. He took me in, and, as much as people think he's a horrible man, he took care of me. I'm not ashamed to say, that because of him, I'm alive."

"But isn't he the one who shot you? Ezra, you——"

Ezra placed a finger to her lips. "He is. But you gotta understand. Garrett grew up rough, too. That old house was passed down to him by his father. I've heard stories about him being tied to a tree and getting his feet burned for stealing a nickel from his daddy.

Sometimes behaviors are inherited. Passed down from generation to generation, and Garrett Monroe was certainly better to me than his father was to him."

She didn't understand why he was defending the guy who shot him in the back. "Tell me about the shooting."

"So, Garrett is a, well, let's just say he's resourceful. His cotton fields were dying, and he had no help to keep them going. He didn't start out being a bad guy. For a couple years after I got there, we did everything we could to keep the fields going. But we just couldn't do it. One day he says to me, let's go for a drive. We were hungry. Our fingers were blistered from picking cotton, and we had only two small bags to show for it. Barely enough to even pay the cost of gas. We drove into town, and he told me to wait in the car. Fifteen minutes later he came back with two bags of groceries, and we ate like kings."

"He robbed a grocery store?"

"I'm really not sure. All's I know is that I was hungry, and he fed me. I had so much respect for him that I told him I wanted to help out, too. The next thing I know, we're driving all the way to Scottsdale to break into homes and cars of the rich. It was like we were Robin Hoods, robbing from the rich to give to the poor… only we were the poor."

"And that was okay with you?" She heard the condemnation in her tone. "I'm sorry."

"No. I get it. And yeah, my conscience weighed heavily on me for a while. But you have to understand. For the longest four years of my life, I mourned the loss of my mother and was treated like an outcast by my own father. Garrett took care of me. He taught me to read and write, gave me life skills, and he fed me. No matter what you say about Garrett Malone, he cared for me like my father never did."

"I understand." She touched his arm. "Go on."

"So, Garrett said if we stick to Scottsdale, we would never get caught. It's a good three hours away, and no one would come looking this far out if we were careful. He said those people could afford to lose a little here and there. But that day, the day he shot me, everything went wrong. Garrett had lost his mind. He wanted to rob a bank at gunpoint. We'd never done anything like that. No one ever got hurt before."

"So, you tried to leave?"

"I got up and walked away. I couldn't be a part of that. I've never seen Garrett kill a man with my own eyes, but I know he has. Mostly people who double-crossed him. So, when I walked out that door, I did it, knowing that I would most likely die."

Charlotte leaned her head on his shoulder. There was so much to take in. So much to understand. Ezra was a criminal, plain and simple, but hadn't she known that?

"You hate me now?"

"No. Of course not. Ezra, you were just a kid. No one would hold that against you."

"Maybe not. But I'm not a kid anymore. I'm a grown man, and I chose to be a part of his gang of hoodlums. I could've walked away at any time."

"And get shot in the back?"

He leaned his head on hers. "Thanks for saving me. I never knew how much I wanted to live until I woke up to your green eyes looking back at me."

"It's never too late to change."

7

―――――

EZRA

"You like my sister, don't you," Cole said as he and Ezra laid the four by four white bathroom tile into the mortar.

Ezra knew the question was coming after Cole had witnessed them holding hands. "I do."

"What are your intentions with her?" Cole laid another tile down and straightened it with a spacer on each side.

"Not sure what you mean." Ezra kept his eyes on spreading mortar.

"I mean, is she just a free place to stay to you or do you care about her?"

Ezra looked up and into the boy's eyes. He respected him for his concern for Charlotte.

"I care for her very much. There's nothing I wouldn't do for her."

"So, if you had to, you would—"

Charlotte popped her head in the doorway. "Cole, Samantha's on the phone."

Cole dropped the tile into place, jumped up, wiped his hands on his pant legs, and rushed out.

"He's got it bad," Charlotte said, looking around. "You guys did great work."

"We're almost finished. Wanna help?" Ezra flicked a clump of mortar at her, and it fell short, hitting the ground.

"Sure." She sat down and flicked it back at him. It landed right on his nose.

"Nice shot." Ezra wiped his nose, smearing the mortar all over his face.

Grabbing a paper towel from the roll next to her, she lifted it to her mouth, wet it with her tongue, and wiped the mortar from his face.

"You drive me crazy when you do that," Ezra teased, swiping his hand in a fan in front of his face.

"What?" Her face turned a deep shade of red. "Wipe the mortar from your nose?"

"Exactly. Makes a man want to cry out in pain."

"I'll show you pain, Ezra McCain," she teased back.

"Get to work, before I kiss you again."

"Promise?" She flirted as she laid another tile into the mortar.

"Never make a promise I can't keep." He leaned in and kissed her. "One for each tile you lay."

"I hope you and Cole had no such arrangement."

"Now you've gone too far." He laughed heartily.

"I'm just teasing. Get some of that mortar spread, I'm waiting for my next kiss."

With each tile laid and spaced, Ezra kissed her. When they were all finished, they stood back and admired their work. "We make a great team, Charlotte Renee."

"We do." She stood on her tiptoes and kissed him again. He pulled her close and allowed his emotions to take over, drowning in her warmth.

"Eh-hmm" a voice came from behind, and they separated like school kids caught making out. Cole looked around them to the bathroom floor. "I see you got the tile finished. Surprising with how distracted you two are with each other."

"Just a celebratory kiss, my man. Tomorrow we can spread the grout, and the next day, we'll install those commodes."

"Yeah," Cole grumbled. "Nice work. I'm going to go tend to the horses."

Cole sidled away with his fists at his sides. It was easy to tell he was not happy about seeing his sister cuddled up in the arms of a villain.

"Maybe you should go talk to him," he said. "I don't want to cause any family issues."

"He'll be okay. He's just worried about me."

Charlotte turned away. He could tell there was something more going on in her brain.

"You agree with him?"

"It's not that. I care for you, Ezra."

"But?"

"But." She turned toward him. "I'm a Christian. God is important to me."

"And He doesn't want you wrapped up in the likes of me?"

"No. No. That's not how God is. I mean, He wants us… Ezra, don't you see? God brought you here. Instead of kissing and flirting with you, I should be telling you about Him."

"Charlotte, I have no use for a God who would let my mother die, allow my father to beat me, and put me in a position to have to steal for my supper."

Tears welled in her eyes. "I don't know why you had to go through that. But can't you see the good in it? It brought you here, didn't it?"

Ezra wiped his hands on his pants and turned. "That's a lot of bad just to get me here. He could've taken an easier route than that."

8

———————

CHARLOTTE

Ezra walked away, leaving Charlotte standing there, watching him. There was nothing she could say to make him understand. Charlotte didn't get it herself. How could she explain to him that in her heart, she felt God had led him to her? It sounded crazy even as she made sense of it in her own head, but Ezra McCain was there for a purpose. And if falling in love was a part of that purpose, she was happy for it. But most of all, she felt God wanted Ezra to come to Him.

Putting her feelings aside, Charlotte went to the stables. She needed to ride, and Samson would be ready for a good trot.

Samson had always been her horse. She'd been only eleven when she'd cared for his mother, Lucy. Charlotte had bathed her, walked her, and spoiled her rotten when she was pregnant with Samson. And when she was foaling, Charlotte spent the entire night in the barn with her, making sure she was okay. She'd wiped the sweat from her brow and whispered sweet words in her ear as Samson's head peeked out. Charlotte had cried tears of joy that day and claimed Samson as her own.

No one could tell her that God was not loving. The miracle of new life was proof of that. Nothing could prove the majesty of God

49

more than the nature all around her. The way the earth spun on its axis, never falling off. The gorgeous sunsets and the stars that shone in the sky. How the wind blew spreading seed, and the bees, pollinating fruit. Everything connected, and if a person looked hard enough, they could see the face of God, smiling, loving, caring for His children.

Saddling up her horse, she took him out. She mounted him and gently squeezed his sides, prompting him to move forward. Clicking her mouth, she nudged him into a canter. Soon he was galloping through the trail and down to the river. The hot wind bit at her face, but she didn't care. She needed to talk to God, and when she was out in the open, just her and Samson, she was better at listening.

Samson stopped at the river, and she climbed down from the saddle as he went to the water to drink. She sat on the bank and poured out her heart to God. Asking Him to change things for Ezra and for her. And, as much as it pained her, she asked Him to transform the heart of Garrett Malone. People didn't change easily, but with God, all things were possible.

The sound of hooves came up from behind, and Charlotte looked up. It was Cole.

"What are you doing out here?" she asked.

Cole jumped down and led his horse to drink at the river next to Samson. Sitting down next to her, he said. "I thought this is where you'd be. I wanted to speak to you."

"It couldn't wait?"

"Well, it seems lately you're never alone."

"Cole, I know what you're going to say, and there's no need to worry."

"I *am* worried. You and Ezra are getting too close." He put a hand on her back. "Charlie, I'm afraid what might happen. Garrett Malone is a dangerous man. And Ezra, how well do you know him?"

Charlotte turned away from him. She didn't believe that Ezra was dangerous, but she agreed that his presence could cause serious issues for them. She hadn't planned on falling for him, it just happened. She worried that she was falling for the first man that showed her attention, but in her heart, she felt she'd loved Ezra from the first time they'd met.

"I'm not trying to be critical, sis. I just want you to be cautious."

"I know. I get it. Thank you for looking out for me."

"Do you love him?"

Tears welled in her eyes. She wanted to tell him emphatically that she didn't but she couldn't. The truth was, she *was* falling in love with Ezra McCain. She nodded silently and wiped her tears.

Cole put his arm around her shoulders. Something he rarely did. "We'll figure it out. And for what it's worth, I think he's an okay guy. It's just that, I feel like——"

"Danger follows him. I know. But he's had a rough life. God still does miracles, doesn't He Cole?" For the first time in her life, she didn't feel like the big sister anymore. She wanted desperately for Cole to give her the answers she sought.

"Yeah, sure He does." He squeezed her shoulder. "But you don't. You can't go trying to change a person into who you want them to be."

"But we can help him, can't we? Isn't that what we're supposed to do? Be a light to the world?"

"Sure. Yeah. But you're not just being a light. You're falling in love. Dad said we cannot be unequally yoked, that means——"

"I know what it means, Cole. But how can I stop what I feel? You know what I'm talking about. I'm sure you feel the same way for Samantha."

"Samantha *is* a Christian, though."

"But what if she wasn't, Cole? What if you fell in love with her and she wasn't a Christian? Could you stop loving her just like that?"

"I don't know. I don't have all the answers, and I'm not telling you to turn off your feelings, just be careful. God can do anything. But a person has to be willing."

"When did you grow up? A couple of days ago you were carrying frogs in your pocket and eating smiley face pancakes."

Cole laughed heartily for a moment. Then he became serious. "When Dad died, I knew I had to step up. I was too young to take his place, but I felt the burden all the same. We're going to make it, Charlie. I know we will."

But will Ezra?

He was her heart's desire. She could be happy spending the rest of her life with him. "Yeah. We will."

"Hey, I didn't come out here to get on your case. I actually came out to tell you we have riders this evening. Got the call right before I came."

"That's great." She tried to sound upbeat but couldn't seem to muster the excitement. Riders kept them above ground, paid for the electricity, and fed them. Things hadn't gotten complicated in her heart until Ezra had shown up.

"Let's go. We need to get the horses ready." He patted her back and stood. "Things will work out how God intends them to."

"Right." But God didn't always work the way she wanted Him to. If He did, she'd still have her parents instead of the heavy burden she carried. She'd be a vet, caring for other people's animals, not struggling to keep her head above water. God had a purpose, that she had no doubt, she just didn't understand it.

Charlotte stood warily and mounted Samson. She'd just have to trust God.

9

EZRA

It had been three weeks since Ezra had been living with Charlotte and Cole, and though he'd vowed to leave after only a couple of days, the news of Garrett's arrest had brought him a small amount of peace.

Cole and Ezra had finished grouting the bathroom tiles and installed the toilets. They had gotten three of the five rooms ready, one of which he insisted on living in. He didn't like the way Cole watched his every move around his sister, but Ezra didn't blame him. He'd earn his keep, and at the first sign of danger, he'd be there to protect them.

"We have our first lodgers," Charlotte said as she walked behind the store where he was sanding down another dresser for the fourth room.

"Oh yeah? That's great. When do they arrive?"

"Well, that's kind of the problem. They're coming tomorrow, and they want three rooms. It's a group of people."

"No problem. I can take one of the unfurnished rooms."

"Are you sure? You're welcome to sleep on the couch."

"No. It'll be fine. I don't want to impose on you."

"I don't think the hard floor will be great on your shoulder."

He was still having trouble with arm movements, and a bit of pain here and there, but other than that, it seemed to be healing fine. "It won't be a problem. This dresser will be finished soon, and I was thinking of grabbing a cot from the bunkhouse."

"Those things are probably old and rotted. Who knows what disease they may carry?"

"I looked at them, and you're right, they're too small for the guests, but the base is actually a plastic mesh, and the frame is fine. It'll be fine for me. With a couple of blankets, I'll sleep like a baby."

Charlotte gave him a hesitant look and then nodded her agreement. "I guess so."

"Hey, you have to set a good example for your brother, right?"

"What do you mean?"

"Well, he said you agreed to allow his girlfriend to come and stay for a week."

"Yeah."

"Then, it's only fair that if she has to stay in a guest room, then so do I."

As soon as his meaning hit her, she blushed. "Wait… you're not… are we—"

He laughed as she tried to speak her mind, only it appeared she didn't know what that was. Over the weeks she had grown on him, and by the way she'd stammered, he had a feeling he was growing on her, too.

Recently, she'd been keeping more of a distance from him. After their talk about God, Ezra understood her hesitance. They'd spent a good deal of time getting to know each other. Then suddenly it stopped. No more evening walks. The intimacy they'd shared had been converted into something of a friendship. Not for him. He still cared for her deeply. But she was going through some kind of inner struggle, and he allowed her to it. He cared for her too much to push her into something she didn't want. Sometimes he was so down, he couldn't see the light through the darkness. That was no way to live. He refused to bring her down with him. She deserved so much more than he offered. He wanted to be brave like those men in the movies, who did what was best for the girl and left. He had to find a way to be that man. To leave her because he loved her.

"Seriously, though. I think it may be dangerous for me to stay here at all. Garrett——"

"You said it yourself, he's in jail. Ezra, you've been so much of a help here. We couldn't have gotten those rooms ready without you."

Garrett wouldn't be in jail for long. He never was, and when he got out, he would come after him. But this, he couldn't tell her. So instead, he gave her another truth. "But you could use the extra room for guests. I don't want to hinder your sales."

"It's not even ready yet. And you more than earn your keep."

Ezra stared at her for a moment, wishing he were braver than his words. "I'm sorry, Charlotte. As much as I'd like to stay, I have to be moving on. It's just something I have to do."

The sadness in her eyes just about killed him.

"I understand. When will you leave?"

"Soon. But while I'm here, maybe you could teach me a thing or two about the ranch?"

Charlotte turned away, but not before a tear slid down her cheek. "Yeah, sure."

"Hey, don't cry." He took her hand and pulled her toward him.

She slipped into his arms easily and laid her head on his uninjured shoulder. "I just don't want you to leave. I feel so safe with you here."

He lowered his head to her strawberry-blond hair. A waft of flowery scent tickled his senses, reminding him of how much he stood to lose by staying there. Holding her at arm's length, he wanted to tell her he'd never leave, but to keep her safe, he had to. "One day, I'll get all this worked out, and I'll come back."

Charlotte turned from him and headed up the dirt path to the stables. It crushed him to see her leave.

A valiant knight, he was not. But for the first time in his life, he wanted to do what was right.

10

———————————

CHARLOTTE

Charlotte brushed Samson down as her thoughts spun around in her head. She understood why he thought he had to leave, but she didn't want him to go. How would he be safe out there? His shoulder was healing better than expected, but where would he go? What would he do? Her feelings were growing for him each day, and she feared that if he left, he would never come back.

The stable door opened, and Charlotte looked back. Ezra stood in the doorway, his long shadow almost reaching her.

He walked toward her. With each step, she thought her heart might break. When he was so close to her that she could feel the heat from his body, he spoke. "How about that lesson?"

"What's the point. You're leaving, right?" She couldn't help sounding upset. She was.

"Not right now, I'm not. You said you'd teach me about the ranch. I want to learn."

"For when you come back?"

He took her chin in his hand and lifted her head to his. "I will come back, Charlotte. That is if you want me to."

She didn't believe him. Once he was gone, he'd stay gone. But still, she obliged him. "Of course, I do. What do you want to learn?"

"Can you teach me how to ride?"

With that, she smiled. "I don't know if you're ready for that. Your arm—"

"My arm is fine. Hardly feel any pain at all. Teach me to ride, Charlotte."

"You asked for it."

She decided on Noel, a Morgan that was born on Christmas morning many years ago, for Ezra to ride. She was a very tame and gentle horse. One she usually used for the kids because she was older and needed very little instruction. She bridled both horses and handed Noel's reins to Ezra. She took Samson's, and they led the horses outside.

"Grab the third saddle and blanket," she said, pointing to the bench just inside the stable door.

Charlotte looked for signs of weakness in his shoulder, and she noticed a slight wince as he lifted the saddle and brought it to her. She had no intent on damaging his shoulder anymore, but something inside nagged at her. If he were hurt, he wouldn't leave. She set that awful thought aside. Was she that desperate she'd wish him hurt just to make him stay longer? Besides, there was still the matter of his lack of belief. She couldn't entertain a life with him if he were not a Christian. Not that it made him less valuable, but it was important that they share the same beliefs.

She showed him how to place the saddle correctly on top of Noel and then grabbed Samson's saddle.

Ezra's face flushed as if being that close to a horse terrified him.

"You sure you want to learn?" she asked. "Noel is one of our gentlest Morgans."

"Yeah, of course, I do," he answered, but his face didn't send the same message.

"Okay then. First lesson. You're in charge of the horse. If you show fear, Noel will sense it. She's a good girl, but some of the others, like Samson here, if he thinks for a second he can get away with acting up, he will." She patted Samson on the neck. "So, you're the boss."

"Got it."

"Okay, then. Lesson two — how to properly secure a saddle," she said.

Charlotte explained what each part of the saddle was for and the importance of each.

She secured Samson's saddle, instructing Ezra to do the same. "Make sure you pull the cinch strap tight," she said as she secured Samson. "But not too tight. She still needs to breathe."

Ezra did as told.

"Now link it through the ring and tie a T-knot."

As if he'd done it all before, Ezra pulled it through and tied the knot perfectly.

"Fast learner. Ready to ride?"

Ezra's Adam's apple bobbed up and down as he gulped visibly. She pretended not to notice.

"Put your foot in the stirrup like this and heave your other leg over the saddle." She climbed on top of Samson with little effort. She'd been riding all her life.

Ezra lifted a leg, and Noel moved. Ezra backed away. "I don't think she likes me."

"Nonsense. Noel can sense your insecurity. Remember. You're in charge. Approach her with confidence."

"Confidence?" Ezra let out a laugh. "Give me a second, I have to find it."

Charlotte giggled. "Let me help you." She got down from Samson and came around to Noel. "Hey, girl. This is Ezra," she spoke into the Morgan's ear. "He's okay." She gave Noel a carrot to distract her. It was very unlike her to be anything but gentle, but Ezra's fear was so strong, she could smell it herself.

"Maybe we should switch. I don't think she likes me."

Charlotte laughed again. "She barely moved, Ezra. Give it another try."

Ezra put his foot in the stirrup and lifted himself on top, this time without effort. He let out a huge grin as if he'd accomplished a significant task. She clapped and cheered for him as he sat in the saddle.

"Now put both feet in the stirrups and hold the reins," she said, steadying Noel as she would for a small child.

Ezra did as she told him. She gave him instructions on how to lightly prod the horse forward with his feet and how to pull on the reins when he wanted her to stop. Once satisfied, she got back on Samson.

"The trail is plenty big to ride side by side. Just keep Noel next to Samson, and he will do most of the guiding."

Ezra nodded, but as Noel moved forward, the saddle began to slide sideways in her direction. Before she could acknowledge the fact that the saddle was not on tight enough, the entire saddle slipped further. She jumped down as the seat flew to the side and Ezra hit the ground. Spooked, Noel's foot nearly came down on top of his chest. Noel backed away smartly.

"Are you okay? I should have checked your saddle before you mounted her."

Ezra let out a groan and held his damaged shoulder. "I think I'm okay."

She helped him to his feet. "Are you sure? Maybe we should save it for another day."

"No, I'm fine." His face showed he was in pain, but he was acting tough.

"Are you sure?" Guilt immediately hit her for her earlier thought. She didn't want to damage his shoulder more. It was only an instant thought she'd brushed away quickly.

"Maybe you should tighten the saddle this time."

Charlotte looked at him for a long while as he dusted himself off. Her instinct was to tell him no, the lesson was over, but her experience told her that the only way to conquer fear was to get back on. "You sure you're not hurt?" she asked.

"A little pain, but I don't think it did any damage."

Charlotte re-saddled Noel, making sure everything was completed properly. Grabbing the saddle horn, she pulled on it to make sure it would not slide again. Kicking herself for not checking it before he'd mounted the first time, she rubbed Noel's muzzle. "Sorry about that, girl."

"You're telling her you're sorry? I'm the one who fell." He chuckled.

"He's an amateur, Noel. Don't listen to him."

Ezra laughed harder. "You got that right."

"Okay. You ready to try again?" Charlotte searched for pain in his eyes but found nothing but amusement.

"Let's do it. Me and Noel are thoroughly acquainted." Ezra placed his foot in the stirrups and climbed back on.

Charlotte shook her head and mounted Samson. Together they took the trail. After a while, Ezra seemed to enjoy the ride more than she expected. The fear she saw earlier was nowhere around. He was a natural. Confident and cool. Of course, Samson and Noel knew the trail by heart. They'd walked it many times over and took every turn with a nice leisurely pace.

"What do you think?" Charlotte asked.

"I like it." He patted the nape of Noel's neck. "I think we're friends."

They rode the trail to the end and dismounted to let the horses drink from the river. Ezra walked around shaking out the noticeable stiffness from his legs.

"I think they're stuck this way." He tried to straighten his legs.

"Sore?"

Ezra put a hand on her shoulder. "A little. But I'd endure anything just to spend more time with you."

Charlotte's heart felt as though it were breaking into pieces. "I don't want you to leave."

He kissed her gently. "I don't want to go. I don't." He rested his forehead against hers. "I'm happy here. Happier than I've ever been in my life. Here, with you, I feel at home."

"Then stay."

"I want to. I really do, Charlotte. But I have to protect you. And every day I'm here, I'm putting you in danger."

11

———

EZRA

At the sound of horses whinnying and hooves vibrating the ground, Ezra sat up straight in bed. He wasn't trained in horsemanship, but since the time he'd been there, he'd never heard such an uproar. The sound of voices and the distinct crack of a whip had him rushing to the window.

"What the…"

It was pitch-black outside, but Ezra could make out the movement of horses along with that of men. Barefoot, Ezra ran out the door to see what all the commotion was. Before he reached the stable, a horse galloped out, raising his front legs, whinnying wildly. Behind him, a man swung at him with a whip. Ezra backed up and hid behind the store wall as the whip made a connection, and the horse reared up his legs.

"Ezra! Come on out! I know you're here!" A man called.

Ezra stared out into the darkness, unable to see anything but shadows. He knew it was Rhett, one of Garrett's men. He'd recognize that accent anywhere. The horse fled away with several others as the men laughed. The time had come to give himself up.

"Yah!" Rhett yelled, scaring the horse into a trot. "Get out of here."

"That'll teach her to go shacking up with outlaws," another man spoke. The voice was surely Bart, another of Monroe's men. "He's probably in there shaking in his boots like the coward he is."

"Come on out, Ezzie! Take it like a man!"

Wanting to go out there and give himself up before any more damage could be done, Ezra took a step forward. What would happen if he did? Would they kill him right there in cold blood?

There was no way he could stand up to them without being killed. They had guns, and he had nothing. Standing up to them would be a death sentence for him and anyone else who got involved. He hesitated. Charlotte was surely awake and watching from the window somewhere, scared to death. No one could sleep through that ruckus. The thought of her watching him being tortured and killed, which would inevitably happen if he made his presence known, stopped him. He couldn't put her through that.

They couldn't know for sure he was there. They could only assume he was. He'd been sure to keep a low profile and had gone nowhere near the Monroe property. The only real reasoning they could've made was if they'd seen Cole pulling him from the desert floor. It was possible, but why wait so long to start trouble?

Rhett and Bart were reckless, and without Garrett to keep them reigned in, they were like hyenas on the hunt. Searching for easy prey.

As much as he wanted to rush out there and stop them, he stayed in place. It took everything he had to keep his feet grounded behind that wall and not go out and get himself killed. Even worse, Charlotte and Cole could be killed for witnessing it. If Garrett had told him once, he'd told them all a thousand times. Leave no witnesses. Until that moment, he'd taken that statement to mean be more stealthily, don't let anyone see you. But those guys, they had no sensitivity to life. They were brutal and angry. Not a good combination.

"Come on out, Ezra!" Bart called. "And we won't hurt the lady!"

Ezra took a step forward. Not that he believed them. It was just the opposite. Charlotte was in the house, and he was right there, only a couple of feet away. If she didn't run out screaming, they might just take him and leave.

The floodlight on the front of the house came on. Ezra jerked his head to the porch. Cole stood there with a shotgun in his hand. Ezra's head whirled at the thought of Cole getting shot. *Please, just go back inside.*

Ezra watched as if everything was happening in slow motion. Before he could take action, Cole raised his weapon and aimed. A shot rang out, and the force of the rifle pushed Cole back. At that same moment, Rhett lit the cloth on a bottle and threw it toward the store. Glass shattered as Rhett fell to the ground.

The flaming bottle crashed inside, igniting everything in sight. Flames immediately licked the inside of the building. Bart ran to Rhett, and half carried, half-dragged him to the vehicle that stood off in the darkness. He dropped him in the back, and they squealed away.

Cole came running from the house. Charlotte was right behind him.

Ezra ran for the hose attached to the spigot just outside the store and flipped it on. Spraying it through the window, he worried he wouldn't be able to put it out before they burned the entire place down.

Charlotte fumbled with the key to the front door. When she finally got it open, she yelled, "Inside, bring the hose in here."

His heart thumping in his chest, Ezra pulled the hose running to the front door, but it stopped short, almost pulling him back to the ground. "It won't reach!"

He ran back to the window. With his bare foot, he busted out the rest of the glass and climbed through. Pain shot through his injured shoulder, but he didn't care. The store was their livelihood. He had to put the fire out before it did too much damage to the store and spread to the lodging rooms.

Ezra sprayed the water on the wooden shelves that had caught fire, soaking everything until there was not a smoldering cinder left in the building.

Charlotte stood at the door, staring into the darkness. An entire assessment of damage could not be made until morning, but it didn't look good. Walking through the soaked ash and debris, Ezra took her in his arms. "I'm sorry. This is all my fault."

"Charlotte!" Cole called from outside. "They've run off all the horses! All except for Samson!"

"God, please, no!" Charlotte cried as she pulled away from him and ran to the barn. "I heard them… I thought…"

Ezra followed her. The foot he'd used to break the glass was wet with blood. He hadn't noticed it earlier, but there was no time to worry about a few cuts when so much else was going on.

"They're gone. The only one left is Samson." Cole jumped on him bareback and rode out of the stable.

"Cole, wait!" Charlotte cried, but he was already gone. She turned to Ezra. "What are we going to do? Why would someone do this?"

"Give me the keys to your truck." Ezra burned with anger. He was ready to take care of it once and for all.

"Why? What are you going to do?"

"I'm going to find out who did this and make them pay." He knew who did it. He had no idea what he would do, but he had to do something.

"Ezra, no."

"Fine. I'll walk." Ezra turned and headed out the door.

"Ezra, please."

He turned back around. "It was Garrett's men, Charlotte. They did this. And it's my fault. They were trying to draw me out, and if I'd have shown my face, they wouldn't have done this to you."

Charlotte stared at him for a long time, her sweet face shadowed in the small hanging light from above.

"They know I'm here. Charlotte, this is all my fault."

"What? How could they know?"

"I told you it was dangerous for me to stay!" His voice was harsh, but the circumstance was serious. "I'm going to take care of this once and for all."

Fear shrouded her face. "Please don't." She touched his shoulder. "Ezra, nothing you can do will undo the damage that is done. And if they see you, they'll… Ezra, please."

She was right. They would kill him, but Ezra wasn't one to take the coward's way out of any situation. He'd grown up hard. He'd learned to take a punch and deliver one back even harder. But then again, he'd never been in love before. Ezra turned away from her.

She touched his arm again. "Please. We need you now more than ever."

"They're not going to stop until I'm dead." He turned and headed for the door.

"So, what are you going to do?" she called out to him. "Just walk in there and think you can fight them all? Ezra, you will lose. I can't—" Ezra turned to see tears streaming down her cheeks. "I don't want to lose you."

He walked the distance back in two strides. Pulling Charlotte into his arms, he allowing her warmth to surround him. He was hurting her, and it was destroying him.

I love you so much, Charlotte.

His heart wanted so much to be the man she needed him to be in that moment. He just didn't know how.

"Okay," he whispered. "I won't go. But I still need your keys."

"Why?" She looked up at him, her face soaked with tears.

He wiped them away, caressing her cheek. "I want to help Cole look for the horses."

"Fine," she said. "Give me a second. I'm going with you. And you should put some shoes on." As she got a clear look at his foot in the light of the stable, she gasped. "Ezra, your foot is cut."

Ezra looked down at his bare feet. The right one was covered in dried blood. "It's okay. Just a couple of cuts."

"No. It's not okay. I'll clean and bandage it for you." She strolled to a workbench and pulled out a first aid kit.

"Charlotte, we have to find the horses."

"We will. Let's get your foot bandaged first."

Ezra sighed. There was no use arguing.

"Have a seat over there. It will only take a minute." She nodded to a stool in the corner.

Ezra limped over, his foot burning. He hadn't felt an ounce of pain while it was going on, but now that his adrenaline was lowering, it was tender.

He sat down, and Charlotte sat on the ground in front of him, lifting his foot into her lap. She grazed her hand over the cuts. "I don't feel any glass inside." With alcohol swabs, she cleaned away the dirt and blood. The feel of her hands on his foot moving so tenderly made him laugh.

"Is something funny?" She looked up at him, her lips pulled up in a grin.

"That tickles. I have very sensitive feet."

"You can take it, tough guy." She continued washing, paying special attention to the middle of his arch. "The horses know where they live. They'll make their way home if we can't find them. I just worry—"

He jerked his foot back with the tickling sensation on his arch. "Stop that! It's not even cut there."

"Oh, sorry. I was thinking about the horses." Her eyes turned serious. "I just hope they're not badly injured." Bandaging up his wound, she dropped his foot gently and stood. "Where are your shoes and socks? I'll get them for you."

"I'll go. I can walk on my heel. You get dressed."

She looked as though she was going to argue, but then nodded. "I'll meet you at the house."

He headed back into his room and slipped on his shoes and socks. His brain warred with his heart over what to do next. His instinct was to go to Garrett's house and set the entire place on fire and watch as it burned to the ground. But for the first time in his life, his heart spoke louder, overpowering his brain.

Ezra went to the house and quietly opened the door to wait inside as Charlotte got ready. As he entered, he found her kneeling on the living room floor, praying. If only he could have what she had. Her faith was so strong that despite all the damage that had been done, she was calling on God to help her.

He stared at the woman on the floor humbling herself before

God and thought about his mother. She'd been a woman just like Charlotte. Her faith hadn't failed her right until the end.

He'd sat next to her in the hospital, praying God would heal her. He was only six and had known little about God but he'd begged the entity to bring his mother back from the illness that had ravaged her body. But no one was listening. Not God. Not the doctors. Not even his father. The day his mother died was the day he'd lost his own will to live. He'd lost trust in humanity. And at such a young age, he'd had to grow up much quicker than he should have. While other kids were playing ball, he was playing hide and seek from his father.

Charlotte rose. In the light of the side-table lamp, Ezra saw the tears that streamed down her face. She was such a compassionate and hardworking woman. She didn't deserve any of this.

If You won't help me, help her.

"Come on. Let's go." Charlotte stood and grabbed onto his hand. Together they walked to the old gray truck.

He couldn't quite understand the woman who didn't seem to have an ounce of anger for the men who tried to burn down her store and ran off her horses. His instinct told him to get revenge. To go after those men and pay them back for what they had done. And there she was, praying instead. He wanted what she had. Peace. He just didn't know how to get it.

12

———————

CHARLOTTE

It had been a long night, and Charlotte was exhausted and emotional. When those men had been out there, she'd watched from the living room window in terror as the men called for Ezra to come out. She'd prayed he wouldn't. She'd begged Cole not to leave the house, but she could not hold him back. Never in her life had she been so scared. Ezra had warned her, but she didn't want to believe him. The anger in his face when he wanted to go after the men, was something she never wanted to see again. She was angry, too. But what good would it do to go after them?

They had found four of the horses. Three others had come back on their own, but Clementine, her pregnant mare, was still missing. She was sick with worry over it. Clementine was due any day, and she was out there somewhere.

"I'm going to go help Cole in the barn." Her words came out unsteadily, and she turned before he could see the emotions welling in her eyes. "Several of the horses have open wounds on them and will need to be…" She broke down in tears at the thought of how those men had brutally beaten the horses for no reason. "How could anyone be so cruel?" She sucked in a breath, taking in their pain.

Arms wrapped around her from behind and she turned and fell into them. The feeling of being held was so overpowering at that moment. She'd spent so much time keeping her distance from him after the talk with Cole, but her heart yearned to be in his embrace. His arms radiated with warmth, sending spikes of electricity into her body.

"I'm so sorry," he spoke into her hair.

She pulled back to look at him, not caring anymore that he saw her pain. "And the lodgers are going to be here tomorrow. I haven't even checked out the store, yet."

"It'll be okay." He pulled the wayward strands of hair away from her wet face. "You go tend to the horses. I'll clean up the store."

"Not only are the horses out of commission for a while, but how can anyone live in those rooms? We're going to lose all the money we put into getting them ready. It wasn't extra. We had nothing extra to spend."

"Let's go look. My room wasn't affected at all by the damage."

"But the horses." She pointed to the stables. "They need care."

"Doc Evans will be here soon. He'll help Cole tend to them."

"Oh, I guess."

Doc Evans was a good vet and would have the horses taken care of in no time, but he didn't live on peanuts. He had to be paid, and they had no more money to shell out. But she would have to do it. She wouldn't dare neglect her horses even if it meant she didn't eat, herself.

They walked toward the store. The shattered window with the garden hose still sitting inside was proof that it had not all just been a nightmare. Black soot covered the outside of the window. And the view inside the store looked bleak.

"Look. The walls are fine." Ezra patted the sooty wall. "Nothing more than smoke and a little of water damage."

"All the souvenirs are ruined. Nothing is salvageable."

"But the structure is sound. A little paint and clean up, and we'll have this place back in order."

Charlotte tried to smile, but she just wasn't feeling it. "Yeah. I guess so."

Even as he tried to convince her it would be okay, she was overwhelmed with what it would take to repair everything. Paint and windows cost more money that they didn't have. They'd get a good chunk from the room rentals, but that was supposed to get her ahead, not push her back.

"Come on. Let's go inside and see what we got."

Ezra headed for the front door, and Charlotte lagged, praying for a miracle to come. Anything short of that and they would be eating cactus candy and jackrabbit for meals.

She entered the store and looked around. It could have been much worse. On the ground, just inside the window, lay the bottle they'd thrown through it.

"Is that what started the fire?" she asked.

"Yep," Ezra said. "It's called a Molotov Cocktail. They fill it with a flammable liquid, throw a cloth of sorts in the top and light it. Once it hits its target, it ignites whatever is around it."

Charlotte shifted. "How do you know so much about it?"

Ezra stared at her for a long moment as if trying to decide what to tell her. But then his eyes turned. "I've read about it."

She had a good idea that Ezra had known much more about how to make such a disastrous concoction than he was letting on. That scared her. What kind of things had he gotten into while being raised by Mr. Monroe?

Grabbing a trash bag from under the counter, Charlotte began shoving the charred remains of her livelihood inside. The water and smoke had done more damage than the actual fire. But it was damaged all the same. All of it would need to be thrown out.

Ezra took the broom from behind the counter and swept the water and debris toward the front door. After his confession of how to make the perfect firebomb, he was quiet. She wanted to speak to him, but the words wouldn't come. Whatever he'd done with that man, it wasn't his fault. He'd been only a boy. That man had corrupted his youth.

There was no use dwelling on what Ezra may or may not have done while living with the old man. The possibilities were unthinkable. She only hoped Ezra hadn't strayed too far to come back from. Anything was possible with God. He could help him. But Ezra didn't seem like the kind of man who relied on God to restore his soul.

Turning her thoughts back to her current situation, she tried to be optimistic. There was nothing they couldn't replace before winter. She'd work extra hard through the summer months to make new items to replace the ruined ones. She just couldn't figure out why God was putting her through all of this.

A memory strolled through her mind as she stuffed the bag full of ruined souvenirs.

She'd been a young girl, and they'd driven out to the feed store to buy hay for the horses. On the side of the road was an accident and a young boy was being pulled from the wreckage.

"Why did God let him get hurt?" she asked. *"What could he have done to anyone?"*

"Things happen that we don't understand," her father said. *"But sometimes, God uses the bad to bring out the good. That man,"* he'd pointed to a man on the side of the road taking a breathalyzer test, *"God might be trying to teach a valuable lesson. You never know what can come from the bad around us. Never give up hope that God is good."*

"Something good will come out of this," she said without even thinking.

Ezra grunted and continued to sweep debris into a pile. "What time are the visitors supposed to be here?"

"In a couple of hours. But even if the rooms don't smell of smoke, they won't be able to ride. I'll most likely have to refund their deposit and send them on their way." As much as she tried to see the good in all of it, her hope was waning.

"Maybe not. If we get the firepit going, we could at least entertain them."

"Yeah, maybe. We'll just have to see."

"I'll get that glass removed, and the window boarded up. It won't look good, but at least it will keep the critters out."

Charlotte looked around the store. Trying to keep a friendly attitude, she said, "Ever worked with wood?"

"As in?"

"You know, trinkets and things. Cole is good at carving. I thought maybe you could help him make some more before winter?"

"Never done that sort of thing, but I'm willing to learn as much as I can to help out." He shoved a shard of glass into a bag.

"Maybe some easier ones at first. That is unless you want me to show you how to sew."

Ezra chuckled. "I think I'll stick with the wood."

"One day I'd like to be able to afford the plush fur to make real stuffed animals. All I can afford now is cloth, but they sell okay."

"One day you will."

"You think so?"

He turned to her, and his face softened. "Charlotte, you pray at every meal, you do everything right, and I saw you last night. When I wanted to go burn that house down, you were praying. You don't believe God will make sure you get all your heart desires?"

What her heart truly desired was him. "It doesn't always work that way, Ezra. God gives us what we need, not always what we want."

Ezra huffed and continued to shove glass into the bag. She knew he didn't understand. She didn't understand it sometimes either. But as hard as it was, she would continue to believe her father's words. She would never give up hope that God had a bigger plan in all of it. If plush fur was not a part of that plan, that was the least of her worries.

Reaching down, she picked up one of Cole's resin scorpions. It had survived the fire with only a bit of ash and water on it. Wiping it on her already dirty jeans, she smiled. Things could be worse. They'd made it out with their lives and all, but poor Clementine hadn't come back.

The thought that it could have been the house that burned down instead gave her chills down her spine. Grateful things weren't as bad as they could be, she was determined to see the good in all of it.

The sound of tires crunched in the drive, and Charlotte looked out to see who it was. "It's the vet. I'm going to talk to him."

Cole came out and met Doc Evans halfway. The two of them discussed the horses as she walked toward them. Looking back, she saw Ezra had already removed the glass from the window and was looking out it at them. His face showed he was still plenty angry about the situation. She prayed he didn't do anything crazy. She was angry herself, but anger wouldn't change a thing. It would only spark a war worse than the Hatfield's and the McCoy's. If that happened, someone would die. She rubbed her arms as she continued to meet her brother and the doctor.

She still worried about Clementine and her unborn foal. There were dangers out in the desert that, being so heavy, she might not be able to outrun. But they'd searched high and low and hadn't found her.

She followed as Cole and Doc Evans headed back into the barn to examine the eight remaining horses. Samson was the only one who had gone unharmed, but that was who they were checking out first. Curious, she stepped forward and listened.

"I think he got one of them." Cole lifted Samson's back hoof and pointed to what could have easily been blood. "What do you think, Doc?"

"Looks like it to me. And from the amount, I'd say he got 'em good."

"Probably saved him from getting hurt like the others."

Charlotte went to Samson, and he nuzzled her face. "Good job, boy." She patted his head, pulled a carrot from her pocket, and gave it to him.

"You think we should call the police?" she asked as they examined the other horses.

"You're certainly within your right to do so, but I worry it may only cause more trouble," Doc Evans answered. "People in these parts live here for the peace and quiet. But if this is who you think it is, you might just be in for more than you bargained for. Is that boy still here?"

"Ezra?" He was hardly a boy.

"That's the one." Opening his bag, he pulled out a salve and coated the wound he'd just cleaned on one of the other horses.

"He is. He's been so helpful to us."

13

———

EZRA

Finished cleaning the debris from the store, Ezra grabbed two full bags of trash and headed over to the bin behind the stable to dispose of them and check on Charlotte before grabbing the mop and bucket to scrub the floors. The woman amazed him at just how strong she was through all of it.

He stopped just outside the stable door when he heard the doctor speaking.

"Helpful or not, believe me when I say that him being here is not doing you any grand favors. Whatever he did to rile up Mr. Monroe, I think you're getting the backlash from it."

"Ezra has been a great help since he's been…"

Ezra dumped the bags into the bin and went back to the house. Grabbing the mop and bucket, he stormed back to the store.

The doctor spoke a truth that burned him to his very core. If Ezra had never stayed with them, Garrett and his cronies would not be trying to take revenge on them.

He loaded the mop with soapy water and cleaned the floors. All the while he made plans to take revenge on Garrett and his crew. Charlotte may have her faith. He had nothing but himself. And he was determined to get justice for her, whether she liked it or not.

"Wow!" Charlotte said, standing in the doorway. "It looks so much better in here. Once we replace the shelves and throw a bit of paint on the walls, no one will ever know."

"And replace the window," Ezra added. He needed to keep his distance from her, or she would know what he was planning, but staying away from Charlotte was like trying to not eat a fresh bowl of ice cream placed in front of him.

"Are you okay?" she asked. "You seem distant."

"Just got a lot on my mind. How are the horses?"

"No actual damage done. A good number of wounds, but those will heal. Doc saw nothing else out of order."

Except for me.

Ezra couldn't blame the man. He was only looking out for Charlotte and Cole. Still, it burned him that he was the problem. As much as he wanted to stay, it was time to go.

"Ezra, you can't blame yourself for this. You didn't cause this to happen."

"No?" he shot back a little too snippy. "And how do you figure that? They came here looking for me."

"Yeah, I get that." She drew closer. "But you did the right thing. Garrett wanted you to do something that was not right. You had every reason to leave."

"I'm so glad you see it that way. But Charlotte, you don't know them like I do. They are not reasonable people. None of this will stop until I leave." *Or am buried six feet under.* "People like Garrett don't just walk away. And besides, that wasn't the first time Garrett asked me to do something I didn't want to do. Now suddenly I have a conscience about it?"

Charlotte touched his arm. "Just because you did those things before, doesn't mean you have to keep doing them. Besides, you said it yourself. Garrett has gone off the deep end. Stealing from others is wrong, but someone will get hurt if he tries to rob a bank. You did the right thing."

He wanted to ask her why she thought she knew him so well. Why she felt that he was an upright man for walking away. He wasn't. He'd have continued to rob and pillage with them for as long as he had to. It was the only way he knew. Like it or not, Ezra was not a good guy.

"I better get this mop put away." He turned away from her. "I'm sorry for all the trouble I caused."

When he turned back around, Charlotte was gone. He looked out the window to see her storming up to the house. Good. If she hated him, it would make what he had to do much easier. He grabbed the water bucket, wishing he was a different man. Trudging back to the stable, he ran into Doc Evans who was just coming out.

"Ezra." Doc nodded.

"Doc." Ezra nodded back.

There was nothing to say. Everyone, including himself, knew he should not be there. All except for Charlotte, that was. Soon she would see the light.

14

CHARLOTTE

harlotte stomped back up to the house. She was so angry with the man she could scream. Why did he insist he was such a bad guy when she knew he wasn't? She did know him, didn't she? They'd spent so much time together that she felt like she did. Maybe she was wrong, and he was right. He was a villain, an outlaw, and could never change.

That wasn't what she saw in him, though. She saw a caring man who was damaged. She wanted to heal him, but there was only One who could do that and Ezra had to be willing. That was where Ezra's issue lied. No one could help him until he made a step in the right direction.

Busying herself with preparing the evening meal, Charlotte prayed for Ezra. God was his only hope. She pulled an onion from the refrigerator and knife from the drawer. She set out the cutting board and diced the onions.

"He has to leave." Cole's voice startled her, and she almost cut her finger.

She looked up to see him standing in the doorway. "Who?" It was a stupid question, and she knew it.

"Ezra. We can have no more problems here. He has to go. You need to tell him."

Charlotte continued to cut her onion, being careful not to slice her finger off. "It's not Ezra's fault, and you know it."

"I don't care whose fault it is. You can't allow him to stay here. It's dangerous. We have guests coming soon. What would they say about people coming in the middle of the night, scaring the daylights out of them? And besides, why haven't we called the police like normal people?"

He was right. They should have called the Sheriff. They should have reported the incident and allowed them to take care of it. She was not equipped to handle the situation. She wanted to protect Ezra, but at what cost?

"Are you listening to me?" Cole walked closer.

Charlotte looked up, tears stinging her eyes. "I don't want him to leave."

"Are you crying?" He touched her arm. "I know this is hard, but we just can't afford this kind of drama."

"It's the onions." Charlotte wiped her eyes on her shirt. There was no way Cole would believe that her tears were due solely to cutting onions. "Can I ask you a question?"

"Sure." Cole sat on the barstool at the counter.

"Do you think people can change?"

"Aw, come on. Let's not go there. This is not about how good or bad a guy you think he is. It's about making sure we are safe. All of us, the horses, our riders, our lodging guests. Charlotte, I'm not saying he's a bad guy. I'm saying he brings trouble. We can't afford that right now. You said it yourself, we are barely getting by. How will we make it if Monroe's men are scaring off all of our customers?"

"Yeah." She swiped at her eyes again. The onions *were* getting to her. "It's just that I feel like you found him for a reason. Like there's a purpose in him being here."

"I found him because he was lying half-dead in the dirt. There's no other reason, Charlotte."

She didn't agree, and as long as she was the older sister, she wouldn't allow Cole to dictate terms. Her father had trained her in every aspect of the ranch, and ultimately, she was in charge. "I'll give it some thought."

Cole raised his hands in defeat.

"What?" She set down her knife. "If you were in his situation, with everyone telling him what a rotten person he is for being raised by a man who made him do… unlawful things, wouldn't you want one person in your corner? Just one, Cole. One person who believed in you. Trusted you. Let you know you can turn your life around and make something of it?"

Cole stared at her, surprise lighting his face.

"Well. Wouldn't you? Everyone needs someone to believe in them."

"Fine. But when everything falls apart, don't forget I told you so."

"I won't. And if I do, I'm sure you will remind me."

Cole turned away. "Right. If I'm alive to."

15

EZRA

Ezra laid in his bed, waiting out the quiet storm in his brain. No matter how he ran through the series of events that started when he walked out of Garrett's house, he just couldn't seem to do anything but blame himself.

Rhett and Bart were trying to do one single thing. Draw him out. He understood that fully, but guilt overcame him like a rushing river. If only he'd have surrendered himself to them before the damage was done, none of it would have happened. That thought set in his chest like a weight.

He was to blame for the injury of their horses and destruction of their store. What they would have done to him, if he'd just come out and given himself up, he was sure he didn't want to know, but it would've been better to let them.

He'd tried to talk himself out of it several times over the day, but each time, he thought of how much worse the situation could have been, the anger sunk deeper and deeper into his bones. Garrett needed to be stopped. The next time, something might happen to Charlotte. That was something he couldn't reckon in his mind. The only way to stop a man like that was death. With Garrett being in jail, there was no chance of that. Still, it wouldn't keep Ezra from taking his revenge.

He allowed that anger to stew deep inside, consuming him with what he needed to do. He closed his eyes.

"You're weak, boy," his father's voice entered his mind. *"I'll teach you to let that punk push you around."* The belt came out, and Ezra was beaten until he was nothing but a crying, bloody mess lying on the kitchen floor.

His father was wrong. He was not weak. He'd never killed a man before in his life, but he'd learned to defend himself. Garrett wouldn't be there, but his men would. Without them, he was nothing but a bitter old man.

Sliding from his bed, his shoulder reminded him that he was still not fully healed. And also, that Garrett had been the one to put a bullet through it. He hadn't killed him as he thought he would, but it wasn't for lack of trying.

Ezra dressed, slipped on his work boots, tied them tight, and unlocked the door. The moment he stepped outside, he was assaulted by darkness. The temperatures were still in the high nineties even in the middle of the night. That was normal. Especially right before the monsoons hit. Looking up to the sky, there was not a cloud around. Good. He wanted nothing to hinder the fire before Garrett's men burned for their sins.

He knew his anger was not good. It hadn't suited his father well, and wouldn't do him any favors either. But as he thought of all the things Garrett had made him do, he reasoned with himself that he was nothing like him. An eye for an eye. Wasn't that what the Bible said?

Setting his mind to do what he had to do before he backed out, he went to the stable. It was much bigger than what was needed for the handful of horses they currently had. As a boy, peeking through the same structure, he'd seen more horses than he could ever count. He'd been amazed at how many there were and would sit outside the back window and count them until Charlotte arrived. Every morning, without change, the entire family would come and care for their horses. He'd been so envious of the love and camaraderie between them, but most of all, he just wanted to see that messy, strawberry-blonde who had captured his heart.

Shaking his head of the memory, he walked to the furthest part of the structure where horses were no longer kept. He removed one of the short hoses that connected the troughs to the piping used to water the horses. Checking the length, he decided it was perfect for what he needed to do.

Being careful not to set off the floodlights at the front of the house, he made his way to the truck. Grabbing the red plastic fuel container from the bed, he siphoned the gas from the tank and took off toward Garrett's house.

The journey through the dark was longer than it had been as a boy when he'd snuck out just before dawn, right under Garrett's nose. The trail, he knew by heart.

The house was dark inside, all but one light in the kitchen where the figures of three men sat. Ezra set the container down and drew closer. Shock settled in his brain as he registered the figure of an old man tipping back in his chair, his feet propped up on the rickety old table, his hands resting casually behind his head.

The anger that had burned down on his way there was refueled. He sauntered to the window to get a closer look. The night was dark. No one would see him.

Across from Garrett sat Rhett, his face bruised and red. The clear shape of a horseshoe was embedded on the side of his face, and his leg was bandaged. Most likely, that was where Cole had shot him.

"You think I don't deserve revenge for what that horse did to me? And that fool boy shot me in the leg," he said. "I gots no problem with going back there and killing every one of them."

"You ain't going nowhere. I already told you to stay away from that ranch, but you had to run about like a skunk spreading stink all over the doggone place."

"Well, you was laid up in jail, and we got antsy. If it weren't for Ezra, we'd a been done and finished that bank job."

"Ezra is dead. I told you, I shot him in the head." Garrett's eyes showed distinct remorse.

"Where's the body, then? I don't believe you'd kill him, Garrett. I think you're getting weak in your old age."

Garrett stood so abruptly that his chair fell over backward. He grabbed Rhett by the neck, lifted him from his chair, and spit in his face. "You ever talk to me that way again, and I'll kill you, too." Letting go of him, he shoved him back in his chair so hard that it tipped over backward. Rhett landed on the floor, covering his face.

"Ain't a one of you worth the time I spent to train you." Garrett kicked at Rhett's feet. "Ezra was the only one of you worth his salt, and he's dead. If you wanna join him, you just say the word." Garrett held his hand on the butt of his gun still holstered to his waist. His fingers turning white.

Rhett scrambled to his feet, his hands in the air, his face white as a ghost. "Okay, okay, just take your hand off that gun. We ain't got no beef."

"Mention that boy one more time, and you'll be laying in the cold hard ground with him. If that ain't before the coyotes get you first."

"Okay. Okay. I get it." Rhett raised his hands.

"And you!" He turned to Bart. "This was all your idea, weren't it?"

A visible fear came over Bart's face. "It was Rhett's idea. He wanted to scare Ezra out. Make em pay for messing up the bank job."

"And what made you think he was there? I told ya I shot him dead, didn't I? You boys hard of hearing?"

"Rhett said he saw horse's hooves leading right from the blood to the west toward the ranch."

"Well, he ain't there. He's dead."

Bart nodded defeat. "Okay, Boss. You say he's dead, then he's dead."

Garrett lifted his gun slightly from the holster. "And you leave that ranch alone. Won't do nothing but get the sheriff on our backs. Y'all ain't got a lick a sense in you."

Rhett and Bart backed down, watching Garrett until he removed his hand from his gun. The fear in their eyes was one Ezra knew first hand. The men turned away, deciding not to answer at all. They were smart to do so.

Ezra backed away from the window and went back to the tree where he'd left his can of gasoline. The look in Garrett's eyes haunted him more than the words he'd spoken. Garrett had to have known that he hadn't killed him. And yet, he was lying to keep him safe.

The words Garrett told him that day came rushing back. *"You're like a son to me."* There was no way he could take revenge against the one person who had pulled him from the gutter and saved his life. There were bad times, Garrett had made him do things that no boy should ever do. Break into houses and cars, stealing from them, and pawning the goods for profit. But he'd always been good to him. Never once laid a hand on him.

His issue was not with Garrett. No, the war waging inside him dealt with his own father. The one who had harmed his psyche more than anything or anyone else. That was the real score that needed to be settled. Garrett was no longer a threat. At least not at the present time.

Ezra grabbed up the gas tank and rushed back to the ranch. Dropping it behind the stables, he headed for the main road into town. He had a score to settle, and he was no longer a little boy who could be beaten into submission.

16

———————

CHARLOTTE

Excited for the new visitors to arrive, Charlotte slipped on a pair of blue jeans, her tan riding blouse, her cowboy boots, and smoothed back her wayward hair. Grabbing the basket of fresh linen and the few items she'd made to brighten up the rooms, she headed out to the guest rooms to get them ready. She'd been praying the entire night that everything would go well and had a good feeling about it.

There were plenty of things she could use to keep their interest during their stay. She'd stayed up late thinking it through. Most people who chose cabins or lodgings such as theirs over the standard motel were out-of-towners who wanted to get in touch with desert life.

A short morning hike on foot would be just as easy to show off the beauty of the land. Of course, it was not as appealing as riding horseback, but the horses were still not ready. Besides the physical damage they'd endured, they were still a bit spooked. Not much, though. It wouldn't be long. Once they healed physically and she put them through a series of tests to be sure they wouldn't spook and throw a rider, she would continue with the trail rides. She had too much respect for the horses to ever put them through more damage.

Opening the first room, she sniffed the air. A slight odor of smoke was present. Pulling out her air freshener, she doused the room. Once the smell met her satisfaction, she made the bed, admiring the work Cole had done on the bed frames. The room was remarkably western looking, and that was what tourists wanted.

After researching the best way to remove the odor of smoke, she'd found that ground coffee beans and baking soda helped to soak up the smell. An idea had come to her the evening before, and she had put together a basket for each room. Inside, she'd placed coffee grounds to serve as a makeshift dirt. She placed small cacti figurines inside and stood back and to see how it looked. The coffee aroma was already filling the room. Smiling, she glanced around. Everything looked perfect.

Moving to the second room, she continued the process. Once finished, she went to the next. By the time she got to the fourth room, the one Ezra was staying in, she stood outside the door, deciding whether to knock. They'd all had a late night. Maybe she should let him sleep.

Cole's words ran through her head. He'd been justified in not wanting Ezra to stay at the ranch. She just couldn't get over the overwhelming feeling that God had placed him in her life for a reason. Of course, there was another reason why Charlotte didn't want him to leave. She loved him.

She glanced at his door once more before turning. She'd let him sleep and go check on the horses. Entering the stable, she went to each of them, giving them all the love she could. One horse, Titus, had been beaten rather severely. Touching the scabbing sore on his backside gently, a tear fell from her eyes. Titus winced, and she went to his head.

Soothing him with a gentle voice, she petted his mane. "It's okay, buddy. You're safe now."

He whinnied softly and nuzzled against her.

"Yeah. That's a good boy." she kissed his soft brown muzzle and pulled a carrot from her pocket. "Here you go, boy."

She spent time with Titus, brushing him down, speaking soothing words in his ear, and avoiding the painful wounds that would no doubt turn into scars.

One by one, she moved to each of the horses. Giving them all special care and love. Doc Evans had said they would be fine in a week or two as long as they were reassured they were safe. She would take every precaution to make sure they received all the love they deserved. She'd lived her entire life around horses. The pain that held her each time she'd had to sell one was unspeakable. But it was necessary for them to survive.

Finished, she headed back to the house. There was only three hours before her visitors were due in and she wanted to make up some fresh lemonade and cookies.

Before she reached the door, a black car pulled up with the word Sheriff written in gold lettering on the side. Had Cole called the police after she'd asked him not to? He'd been furious all day and had gone off many times about the unfairness of it. He'd almost been angrier over it than Ezra, and Cole was not an angry person. He was as gentle as the horses he cared for.

Sighing, she walked over to the vehicle as a tall, dark-skinned man dressed in a khaki uniform got out of his vehicle.

"Ma'am." He nodded. "Looking for Charles Spencer."

"He's my… well, he was my father. He passed away many years back. I'm Charlotte."

"I'm sorry for your loss, ma'am. Are you running this ranch alone?"

"No, sir. It's my brother and me. What can I do for you?"

"There was a fire last night on the Monroe property about three miles east of here. House burned to the ground."

Charlotte covered her mouth. "Is everyone alright? Did they…"

"Apparently there was no one in the house at the time, but —" he glanced at the store and saw the boarded-up window. Walking toward it, he looked inside. "Looks like you suffered some damage, too."

"Yes, sir. Two nights ago, our horses were run off, and a fire started in the store."

"I haven't seen a report on this incident. Is there a reason you didn't call it in?"

Charlotte refused to meet his eyes. How did you explain to an officer of the law that you feared calling them because it would only make matters worse?

Just then Cole walked out of the house. "Hey, what's going on?"

"Cole, uh, this is Officer——" Had the guy introduced himself? She didn't think so.

"Deputy Hale." The Deputy stretched out his hand. Cole took it as he continued. "Hear anything about the Monroe house burning down last night?"

For only a second, Cole's eyes glimmered. "No, sir. Was home in bed. But as you see, we got attacked the night before." He pointed to the boarded-up store.

"That's what your sister was saying. If we got hoodlums running around, we need to take care of it before someone gets hurt. I'd like a full statement as to what happened to your property." The deputy's brow was lit with moisture. "You got insurance on this place?"

"Yes, sir. We haven't reported it yet." Her deductible was so high on the place that paying that alone would break them. There was no use even filing a claim.

"Cole, why don't you take him inside, and get him some water. You know more about it than me." Her primary concern was speaking to Ezra about it. Her heart refused to believe he had anything to do with it, but hadn't he said he would?

"Yeah, sure." Cole gave her an I-told-you-so look and headed for the house.

The officer followed Cole into the house, and Charlotte left for the lodging rooms. She just hoped Ezra hadn't done something stupid.

Knocking on the door, she waited. There was no answer. She knocked again. Still no answer. Maybe Ezra was a heavy sleeper. A blush came over her at the thought of finding him laying on top of the covers with nothing but his underwear, but she pushed it away and wiggled the handle. It was no time for modesty with the sheriff's officer at their door.

The handle turned. It was unlocked. Charlotte opened it just enough to peek her head in and called his name.

The bed was completely empty, the covers ruffled as if he'd been there, but he was not there now. Closing the door back, she went to the stables. She'd just been there, but maybe she had missed him.

God, please don't let him be the one responsible for the Monroe fire.

Her prayer was futile. Either he was, or he wasn't. There was no praying that could change that fact.

Ezra was nowhere to be found. She went up to the house and listened to Cole tell the story of what happened two nights before.

"You say you shot a man?" The deputy scribbled in his note-book. "Where do you think you got him."

"Not sure if I got him or not." He gave Charlotte a wary look. "Everything was crazy. It all happened so fast."

Charlotte could see he worried about shooting a man. He was defending them, but it was still a scary thing. She understood. She'd heard of lawsuits from burglars who got shot entering someone's house. The right to defend oneself was a thin line.

"And that's when they left? Did they take anything? Money? Valuables?"

"No. I don't think so." Cole looked back at Charlotte. "Was there anything missing?"

"They never came into the house or store. I don't know what their intentions were. Maybe Cole scared them off."

The officer wanted to see the horses, so she led him to the stable.

She took him to Titus first. "Please stay back, though. He's a little spooked right now."

Deputy Hale nodded and took pictures from as far back as he could of each of the wounded animals.

As they left the stable, he said, "Your brother here says he didn't get a look at the assailants. Did you happen to see anything?"

"I didn't. All I saw was my store on fire and a dark truck driving off."

"Did you get a license?"

"No, sir. I was trying to save my store from burning down. We spent hours into the night trying to round up the horses. One of them is still missing. She's pregnant. She'll be foaling soon."

The deputy asked for a description of Clementine and told them he would keep an eye out for her. He asked a couple more questions then got back into his vehicle and drove off, leaving dust in his trail.

Charlotte rushed to the henhouse for eggs.

Cole was hot on her tail. "Tell me he didn't start that fire."

Charlotte turned half way there. "He didn't."

"Where is he? How do you know? He talked about it. I heard him."

"He's gone."

"I knew it." Cole whipped off his hat and ran a hand through his sweaty hair. "He did it. We're harboring a criminal. What did I tell you?"

"He's gone, Cole. Let it go." Charlotte continued to the chicken coop.

Still following her, he called, "He better not come back. Charlotte, we could lose everything we've worked for."

Charlotte whipped around. "You think I don't know that?"

"Okay." Cole raised a hand in the air. "Okay. I'm sorry. I'm just worried about all of this."

Charlotte calmed. "I'm worried, too."

Not big on brotherly affection, Cole shifted, running a hand along his light stubble. "I'll go milk the cow. Our visitors should be here soon."

Charlotte nodded and continued her trek to the chickens. With the few they had left, they'd had no choice but to stop eating them. The eggs they produced were the only things keeping them from being the evening meal.

WITH COOKIES MADE, Charlotte looked out to see a van pulling up. Two adults and two children hopped out, checking out the ranch. Charlotte said a short prayer that they would stay after hearing they wouldn't be able to ride and went out to meet them.

Placing her best smile on her face, she greeted them. "Hi! Welcome to C&C Trails. I'm Charlotte, and my brother Cole is out in the stables."

"Hello. It's good to get out of the car." the man said, rubbing the back of his neck. "You're quite a ways from town."

"It's good to have you, Mr. Bell." She shook his hand. "Mrs. Bell."

She always made a point of remembering each adult guest's names to make them feel welcome. "And who are these handsome young men?"

"I'm Charlie," the older boy said while the younger one hid behind his mother's legs. "He's Carl."

Once the introductions were made, Charlie asked, "When can we ride the horses?"

Charlotte gave him a sad smile. "I'm sorry, I didn't call and let you guys know, but the trail rides are closed for a week or two." She looked up at the adults, resolving to be perfectly honest with them. "We had a bit of mayhem here recently. Some horses were harmed, and the store caught on fire. Maybe now is not the best time for you all to stay."

"Really?" Charlie asked. "A real shootout like the one we saw in Tombstone?"

Carl's eyes grew wide as he peeked behind his mother.

"Unfortunately, quite like that. Uh, I can show you the rooms if you like. Each of them has a lock, and I don't think we'll be seeing any more trouble around anytime soon." She tried to keep the sad look from her face as she waited for their decision.

"Well, we're here now. Let's have a look around, and then we can give you an answer."

Charlotte nodded and led them toward the lodging rooms.

Passing their milking cow, Carl asked. "Could we milk her? I never milked a cow before."

Charlotte smiled. It didn't take much for him to come around.

Gemma was as gentle as they came, and she saw no reason not

to let them. "Absolutely. My brother, Cole is the best at teaching. If you promise to listen to him, I'm sure he'll let you. You could even help me gather eggs in the morning."

"Yes!" Charlie's fist flew the air. "Can we, Dad?"

"Sounds like fun."

"We also have one horse who was uninjured. Samson. He's an old, gentle guy who's great with children. I'd love to lead the kids around on him. We also have a hiking trail that leads right up to the river."

With that settled, the boys had all but convinced their parents to allow them to stay.

"This is going to be the best fun ever!" Charlie said as they ran to the chicken coop to see the birds.

"I think it'll be okay," the husband said, turning to his wife. "What do you think?"

"I think getting them out of here now would be a huge battle. Besides, I like the feel of this place."

Charlotte thanked them happily and did her best to assure them there would be no problems. She just hoped that was true.

17

———

EZRA

Ezra stood outside of the home he'd lived in until the age of ten. After spending three hours with the truck driver who had picked him up, listening to him drone on about life on the road and his family back home, Ezra had been ready to get it all over with. But now, standing at his birth father's door, fear washed over him.

"WHAT DID I TELL YA, boy? I know you were into my beer," his father slurred, standing over him with an empty bottle in one hand and a belt in the other.

Ezra shrunk in fear. He hadn't touched his father's stash. He knew better. "No, sir. I didn't touch it."

"You gonna lie to me, Ezz-rah?" His voice slurred with each word. "Am I raising a liar?"

There was no use speaking another word. All he could do was endure the pain that was to come. His father raised his belt and lashed him until Ezra cried out in pain. With a yell, he threw the bottle to the floor, staggered off and fell asleep in the chair.

. . .

EZRA WASN'T that scared little boy anymore. Knocking hard on the door, he was determined to confront the father who left scars on his back and legs. A forever reminder of his cruelty.

A dark-skinned, heavy-set older woman answered the door. She wore a knee-length, flowered dress like his mother used to wear, and her hair was jet-black with a widow's peak of gray streaking through. She smiled at him kindly.

"Can I help you, young man?"

"Uh, hi. My name's Ezra McCain. I used to live . . . my father owned this house all my life. His name was William. William McCain."

"Oh?" The woman stepped outside and closed the door. "Yes, I do believe the man we bought the house from was named McCain. We still get mail for him a time or two."

He sold his house? "About how long ago did you purchase the place? If you don't mind me asking."

"About four years back. Are you looking for him?"

"Yes. My father and I—" Ashamed to tell her his father was an abusive drunk, he went vague. "We had a rough relationship."

"That's too bad." She gave him a sad smile. "To the best of my knowledge, he could no longer take care of the place. I hear they placed him in one of those care homes. Alzheimer's, I think."

"Alzheimer's?" His father was a drunk, but the thought never occurred to Ezra that he would ever lose his faculties. "Do you know where?"

"No. I wasn't privy to that sort of information. Would you like to come in and take a gander on the internet? Don't know much about that old laptop myself."

"No." Ezra was still internalizing the information and had no wish to see the home that had caused him so much anguish. "No, thank you. Uh, thank you for your time."

"Sure. No problem. I hope you find what you're looking for."

Ezra thanked her again and walked back down the sidewalk. In a complete daze, he left the housing development he'd grown up in and took the main road into town. Not even bothering to hitchhike, he walked slowly and methodically.

Once in town, he passed a library. He stopped for a moment and glanced inside. He'd never held a library card, but he had his identification. Regardless of his father's condition, he still wanted to see him.

Heading inside, he filled out the form for a library card, showed his driver's license and set to work on one of the available computers.

First, he looked up Alzheimer's. He read through the long list of symptoms ranging from confusion to a total lack of body function. Where was his father in that stage? Would he be able to talk? Understand? Would he even remember his son or that he had a son?

Pushing the questions away, he searched for facilities that would care for Alzheimer patients in the area. Three came up in his search. He scribbled the addresses of each of them down with a half-sized pencil and a small square of paper.

He went to the desk and asked to use their phone. The lady looked at him as if he was some kind of alien. Everyone in the entire United States had a cell phone, but not Ezra. He'd never had a need for one until that moment.

Shaking her head, she handed him the receiver. He dialed the first number on the list.

18

____

CHARLOTTE

"Well, that was fun," Charlotte said, waving to the vehicle of lodgers as they left the ranch. "I'm exhausted."

For three days, they'd entertained their visitors. She and Cole had taken them on hikes, showed them how to milk cows, gather eggs and pointed out nearly every cactus and tree in the desert. She'd given the boys rides on Samson, and they'd laughed and run around until they were tired.

They'd all laughed heartily when the older boy, Charlie, mentioned he was disappointed he didn't get to see a real live shootout. She was glad there had been no more trouble. Still, she worried about Ezra. She'd not seen him in three days, and although she tried not to, her mind always went back to the worst. Something terrible had happened to him.

"Samantha will be here tonight. I want to run into town, you want to go with me?" Cole asked.

Still undecided about letting Cole have his girlfriend stay on the ranch, she'd given in purely because she didn't have a valid reason to argue. He was a grown man and had agreed Samantha would stay in one of the lodging rooms. What more could she say? If she couldn't be happy, at least he could.

"Sure. Let's go. I want to pick up some paint for the store. The sooner we get that painted, the sooner we can start putting stuff back inside." They'd wiped down the walls and left all the windows and the door open to allow it to air out, and most of the smoke was gone. Charlotte had placed baking soda pouches all over the room as well. Painting was a necessity they couldn't afford to skimp on. It frustrated her that the money that should go back into their savings would be spent on it, but there was nothing she could do about it.

Cole pulled the keys from his pocket. "Let's go then."

She almost came back with a comment about how he hadn't even asked her before he decided he was going. She often forgot that he was an adult and was just as part owner of the ranch as she was. Biting her lip, she staved off the comment and followed him to the truck.

Cole got in and started up the truck as Charlotte climbed up into the passenger seat. It roared to life. She buckled her seatbelt and Cole put the truck in drive. Before they made it out of the driveway, the car coughed and stalled.

"What the—" Cole looked down at the dash. "It's clean empty."

"What do you mean? We had plenty of gas in the tank."

Cole got out and glanced into the truck bed. "Fuel can's gone." He stomped back to the driver's seat and flopped in. "Still think he didn't burn down that house?"

Charlotte looked away. Her eyes roved over the surrounding desert. "I don't know."

"Get on this side. You drive, I'll push." He got out, and Charlotte slid into the driver's seat as Cole pushed the truck backward to the house.

Charlotte put the brake on and climbed down. "Cole, maybe it's not what we think." She was unsure of her own words.

"Shoulda let that guy die in the desert." He stomped off and into the house.

Charlotte stared off at her brother. There was no denying it now. The proof was staring her right in the face. Ezra had taken his revenge. He wasn't the man she thought he was.

"SHE'S HERE." Cole took the porch stairs with one jump, startling Charlotte.

"Guess you're in a better mood," she said, bringing a basket of eggs into the house.

Cole turned to her as Samantha parked her car. "Not a word of this to her. I don't want to scare her."

"She's going to know, Cole."

"I mean about your boyfriend burning down the Monroe house." He turned and walked away.

"You don't know that for sure, Cole," she called, still hoping against hope that she was wrong and it was all a misunderstanding. It was easier than accepting reality.

As Samantha opened her door, Cole brought her into a hug.

Swelling emotions ran through her at the thought of being in Ezra's arms only days before. Where was he?

"Samantha says she'll take us back into town," Cole said as they headed toward her, holding hands. "I told her we'd treat her to dinner."

Charlotte staved off an eye-roll as she walked toward them. They didn't have the money to waste on extravagant dinners. They barely had the extra to buy the paint and a few other supplies they would need. But if it made Cole happy, she'd find a way to save somewhere else.

After a half hour of chatting about Samantha's drive in from Phoenix, they headed back into town. Cole and Samantha held hands and talked in low tones while Charlotte sat in the backseat, desperately worried about Ezra.

Once in town, Cole dropped her off at the fabric store as he and Samantha went to the hardware store to grab paint. All the while, Charlotte's eyes roved through the town. Was Ezra here, somewhere?

She headed to her favorite section. The plush fabric. The store had bolts and bolts of it, but she just couldn't afford to buy it. She rubbed her hand across the soft fur, delighting in its softness. Ezra's words came to her. *"Someday, you will."*

Charlotte took in a deep breath to stave off tears of worry.

Where are you?

Settling on a cheaper cotton fabric, she ordered three yards, grabbed a spool of thread, and paid for her items.

Samantha's car was idling out front when she finished. She hopped in the back, and the three of them went out for an early dinner at a local diner. Feeling like a third wheel, she followed them inside.

A server led them to a table, and they sat down.

"This place is cute. You never find the old rustic look in Phoenix. It's so metropolitan."

Once their meals came, Charlotte was happy to be distracted by the food. She liked Samantha. She seemed like a sweet girl, and she was delighted for Cole. It was just that every time she looked at them together, giving each other that dreamy look, she wished it was her. How had she ended up falling for the bad guy?

"Samantha and I are going to paint the store. We wanted to give you a break." Cole leaned in and kissed Samantha on the cheek and Charlotte could take no more. She had to get away.

"That's great. Oh, I forgot. I've got this flyer I made for the new lodging. I want to post it on the board," Charlotte said, leaving the lovebirds to their dinner. She'd already eaten as much as she could and wasn't very hungry to begin with.

As she passed the countertop diners on her way to the front of the restaurant, a man caught her attention. From the back, he had a husky build, short black hair, and was wearing a t-shirt and jeans. Her heart stopped. It was him.

Not knowing whether to approach him or keep walking, Charlotte stood and watched. The man cut his chicken and lifted the fork to his mouth. Even the way he made those small moves, she was sure it was him. If only she could see his face.

Without another thought, she walked forward and tapped him on the back. "Ezra?"

The stranger turned, giving her a toothless smile. From the

front, he looked nothing like Ezra. His scruffy beard and long nose were proof of that. Not to mention the pockmarks on his face that proved he'd had a rough time with acne as a teenager.

"Well hello, darling. The name's Joe. But you can call me whatever you like."

"So sorry." Charlotte's face heated. "I thought you were someone else."

"Well, that's okay. Feel free to have a seat. I don't bite."

"Uh, no thank you. It was nice talking to you. I have to go."

The stranger let out a guffaw as Charlotte rushed off, heart pounding in her chest, to the corkboard. She posted her flyer and hurried back to her table.

Once she got back, Samantha was handing the bill to the server.

Her heart was still beating double-time as she asked, "What's going on?"

"I told her not to," Cole advised.

"Oh, come on. I'm getting a week's room and board, the least I can do is flip for a little paint and food."

"You paid for the paint, too?"

"It's no big deal, sis. She wanted to." He looked at Samantha adoringly.

"Thank you, Samantha. I appreciate your help," she said as they headed out to the car. "Things are a little tight lately."

At least that was one worry she didn't have to mull over.

"So, I heard. Don't worry one bit. I'm glad to help."

When they were close to home, Charlotte was almost asleep when Cole's voice startled her.

"It's been a week," Cole called back to her. "You ready to test out the horses?"

Charlotte yawned. "Yeah. We'll do it just like Dad taught us."

"And how's that?" Samantha asked.

"We bring them out to the corral and put them through a series of tests. It's rather —" Cole stopped. "Charlotte. Is that Clementine?"

Charlotte looked out toward the flowing San Pedro River. "It's her! Stop the car!"

Samantha hit the brakes hard. Charlotte's seat belt slung her back. She unbuckled it and ran out into the desert. Cole was right behind her.

When they got closer, they slowed down. "Don't spook her," Charlotte whispered.

"Hey, girl." Cole clicked his teeth. "It's okay. It's me, Cole."

Clementine lifted her head in a soft whinny.

"Yeah, that's right. It's just Charlotte and me. You ready to come home, girl?"

Cole walked up to Clementine and Charlotte stayed back while he talked calmly to the horse. "Come on, girl. It's okay." He put his hand out for her to sniff.

Clementine responded to him, and he petted her. "That's a good girl. We've been looking for you for a week."

Charlotte came forward and held out her hand. "Hey, girl. We've missed you. You ready to go home?"

"She has no reins, and we can't ride her being this far along, I'll walk her back."

"I want to come with you. She could foal at any time. We should both be with her."

Cole agreed. He told Samantha they'd meet her at the house and the two of them walked the mare home, gently soothing her the entire way.

Thank you, Lord!

19

—————

EZRA

Ezra sat under the bridge where dozens of homeless people congregated for the evening. The bridge crossed over a wash that in rainy months kept the city from flooding. It was dry most of the year, and that's where many of the homeless came to sleep. It was relatively safe and far enough out of town that the police didn't bother them. Some of them he'd seen as a boy, many of them were new. All of them were hungry.

He'd found out where his father was staying, but he hadn't brought himself to go speak with him yet. With no money, and undecided about meeting his father once again,he closed his eyes as memories surfaced.

"Get out of here, kid!" a man wearing a white apron with crimson blood running down the front called out to him. "Don't let me catch you around here again."

"Can I have a dollar, mister?" Ezra asked boldly. He hadn't eaten in days.

"What do I look like? Go find your family. The streets are no place for a kid."

Ezra turned with a frown and walked away.

"Wait a minute," the butcher called to him. "Where're your parents?"

"My mom's dead. My dad… I ran away."

"How old are you?"

"I'm ten, sir."

The butcher's eyes showed concern. "Now look, you can't stay behind my building. I'm sorry about your mom. Maybe you and your father can work it out? I'm sure he didn't mean ta——"

Angrily, Ezra pulled up his shirt to show the fresh scars.

"Maybe not, then." The butcher reached into his pocket and pulled out a bill. "This is all I got." He handed Ezra a five-dollar bill. "You go down to that bridge just outta town. There are some others out there. They take care of each other. Sleep there at night. You'll be safe there."

Ezra took the money and thanked him.

THE MAN HADN'T CALLED the police that day, and Ezra had been thankful. He knew nothing about life at that time. What if the man had called the police? Would his father have been arrested? Would they have thrown him into some foster care system? How different would his life be if he'd never have met Garrett?

An older man, wearing a US Vet ball cap, limped over to him and sat down. The odor that wafted through the air was one that Ezra knew well. Living on the streets in the dead of summer, everyone smelled bad.

"Haven't seen you around. Tough break?"

"Something like that. How about you?"

"Army, twelve years. After the Iraq war, never been the same. They call it some big fancy word, but basically, I'm all jacked up. Couldn't hold a job for the life of me. After the wife and kids left me, I settled on the streets."

"PTSD?" Ezra asked.

"Something like that. Seems, if even a pin dropped, I was hiding under a table to take cover."

"The army didn't help you? I mean, after you got out?"

"They tried to git me some of that mumbo jumbo counseling, but that stuff, it doesn't work. Them people that sit in their cozy chairs behind their pretty little desks, they ain't ever seen no man get killed."

Ezra chuckled. "I imagine you're right."

"Like I was saying, that lady they set me up with, so thin and frail, she'd about have a conniption when she broke a nail, how was she going to help me?"

"You think a normal person, I mean one who hasn't been in a war, can have PTSD?"

"Why, sure. It's just your brain going all wacko from the suffering. The brain can only take so much before it shuts down. Why? You jump under tables, dodging imaginary bullets, too?" He chuckled as if it were a joke.

"Nah. I was just curious." Although the more he thought about it, the more he wondered about the fear rooted inside his heart. The way his brain had always gone into panic mode that first year after he'd run away. How, for the longest time, he'd duck and cover at the slightest glance. Those were things he'd learned to overcome over the years, but a nagging fear of never being accepted had settled in his heart.

"I'll tell you what saved me from offing myself and just letting it all go, though. It was one of those street preachers. He comes out here every Sunday. Brings us food and usually says a couple of words. Most of the guys, they laugh and carry on after he leaves. I did too at first, but one day his words got to me. He'd said the only right fear was the fear of the Lord. Once I got that settled in my heart, I wanted to learn more. That man, he sat me down, told me it weren't right for me or anyone else to be on the streets, but that God loved me just as much as any other. I gave my heart to Jesus that day."

"Then why are you still here?"

The veteran chuckled. "God ain't no get rich quick plan. I figure he put me here for a reason. I've been through the wringer, that ain't no lie, but I've been able to help a man or two get right with the Lord."

Ezra thought about it some. His mind went back to Charlotte, humbled in prayer. "I thought God watched over His people. What good is it if they still have to suffer?"

"Crazy thing about that. It's not this life that He guarantees happiness. Preacher showed it to me right out of the good book. Says Christians will suffer for His namesake. It's just how it is. Believing in something even after all the suffering and pain, it's healing. Did I tell you ain't had one bad dream since the saving? I may be dirty and old, but I know where I'm going."

"And where is that?"

"I got me the sweetest mansion in Heaven. Sits right on top a hill of the purdiest flowers and long flowing grass. Streets of gold for as far as the eye can see. I figure a couple missed meals now ain't so bad once I get to the feast prepared just for me."

"Sounds like a dream." Ezra shifted. That's where his mother was. She'd told him the same thing. The thought of seeing her again one day laid heavy on him.

"It sure does. But I tell you what. If that preacher is wrong, they'll bury me in some cemetery a rotting corpse, but if he's right, I got my mansion. It ain't about saying the words, it's about believing in something more powerful than yourself. That's what it's about."

"Streets of gold, huh?"

"For as far as the eye can see. And no more worries. It's what He promised. Preacher showed it to me. But there's something more than that. It's a peace that dwells inside of you. He called it the Holy Spirit. And I'll be darned if he weren't right. Got it right here." He pumped his chest.

"Thanks," Ezra answered. It was hard for him to see God differently from what he'd known as a father. A mean tyrant who cared nothing for his child. "You gave me plenty to think about."

"Just doing my job. What's eating you? I know you ain't out here because you want to be. You're young. You could get a job most anywhere."

"I came here to find my father. I found him, but I'm wrestling with whether to have it out with him."

"He weren't so good to ya, was he?"

"No, he wasn't. That was a long time ago, though."

"The past ain't an easy thing to recover from. Best thing to get it behind you is to confront it head-on. I wish I'd done that with my family."

"Yeah." The silence between them grew thick, and Ezra stood. He held out a hand to help the old guy up.

"You go on and face those demons head-on." The veteran patted him on the back. "You'll be the better for it. And don't you forget what I told you about that saving thing. All you gotta do is say it. He knows your heart."

"Thank you, uh… I didn't get your name."

"Stanley."

"Ezra."

"Good Bible name. You're off to an impressive start already."

Ezra grinned. "Yeah."

As they said their goodbyes, Ezra headed back into the city. Words from his mother brought him comfort. He remembered little about her, but her voice came back to him.

"I named you Ezra after the old testament man. He was strong like you. When the Jews returned to Israel, he was instrumental in helping them renew their fellowship with God. You can carry that name with pride, son."

He hadn't thought about those words in ages. He'd never opened the Bible once on his own. His mother thought him strong back then. But when she died, so did his strength.

Ezra stopped at the address where his father was being cared for. It was a two-story stucco building with a sign outside that read — *We Care.* Underneath in smaller words it said, *Nursing Home and Assisted Living.*

Taking a deep breath, Ezra walked up the sidewalk to the front door. He went inside and walked over to the front desk.

"I'm here to see William McCain."

The young woman at the desk smiled. "Are you family?"

Ezra wasn't sure how to answer. He didn't think of the old man as a father anymore and worried if he admitted the truth, they would look down on him for never visiting him. In the end, Ezra settled for the truth. "I'm his son."

"Oh, great. If I can see some ID, I'll get you right back there to see him."

Ezra pulled out his driver's license, showed it to the woman. She looked it over and handed it back.

"Go on and have a seat. I'll get a nurse up here to escort you back."

Ezra sat and stared out the plated glass windows. The thought of seeing his father was a tremendous weight on him. Stanley's words weighed on his heart. What he wouldn't give to have peace. Without a beat, he closed his eyes and prayed. Admitting he'd always believed in God but never accepted Him as ruler of the universe, he asked Him to restore his peace.

I believe what You did for me. Sent Your son to die for my sins. Please give me the peace that Charlotte and Stanley have. I don't want to wander in life anymore.

As he opened his eyes, a woman in light blue scrubs opened the door and led him back. As the Holy Spirit filled his heart, he was ready to meet his father. He knew little about what he'd just done, but it felt right. Freeing.

"They're just sitting down to lunch. You're welcome to join him. The foods not the greatest here, but it's not so bad."

"Thanks."

In the middle of the cafeteria, his father sat in a pair of brown pajamas. His face looked worn and wrinkled, his hair thin and gray. He was no longer the powerful man who ruled with an iron fist.

"William," the nurse called out as they got closer.

His father didn't even look up from the woman who was spoon-feeding him.

"William." The nurse bent down, catching his attention. "You have a visitor."

His father looked at him, his eyes blank. "Who's this."

"William, this is your son, Ezra."

Confusion settled in his eyes for a moment, and then he turned back to the assistant who was feeding him.

"He's in the late stages of Alzheimer's. I'm sorry, but he may have no recollection of you."

Ezra nodded. "Yeah, I kind of figured that."

Ezra sat across from him and watched as his father robotically opened his mouth for the woman feeding him. His old, liver-spotted hands tremored on the table.

"Dad?" Ezra said.

His father glanced at him, mumbled something, and then turned back to the nurse for another bite.

"All done, William. Are you ready to go back to your room?"

He didn't answer.

"He's better on some days than others. This morning is one of those worse days. Sometimes he finds clarity, but it doesn't last long."

"He might remember me?"

"At some point. But like I said, it comes and goes. So, you're William's son?"

"Yes."

The girl gave him a sad smile. "I've heard a lot about you. In bits and pieces only. Seems he thought you were… uh… he talks a bit about his son dying. Did you have a brother that passed?"

"No. It was just me."

"Would you like to push him to his room?" she asked as she dabbed at his father's chin. "I'll give you some time alone with him if you like."

Ezra stood and went around to the back of his father's wheelchair. The nurse unlocked the wheels, and he followed her down the hallway. It seemed strange to be in the same room with the father who had ruined his life, and yet, he couldn't bring himself to hold it against him. He'd set out to confront him. Get everything off his chest and have it out. He'd rehearsed repeatedly how he would blame him for his lifelong struggles. But pushing his father down the hallway, he couldn't find the anger that had always taken over his heart.

It didn't matter. The old man didn't have the capacity to understand, anyway. Even if he'd have gone off on him, his father would not understand a word he'd said.

The nurse stopped at a room and signaled for Ezra to push him in.

Once inside the room, she helped him stand as he wobbled to the bed, turned, and sat down on the edge. "It's his naptime, but you're welcome to stay."

His father pushed himself backward on the bed and leaned back. The nurse lifted the side rail and turned. Before she could speak to him, a small phone on her hip rang. "Excuse me for a moment." She walked out of the room, leaving Ezra alone with his father.

Ezra stared at his father for a long time. It appeared he didn't know he was even there.

And then he spoke. "Ezra."

Ezra jumped up. "Dad?"

"Ezra. Read me the book of Ezra." He pointed a shaky finger to the Bible on the table by his bed.

"You know, I had a son named Ezra. He's gone."

Ezra picked up the Bible in his own shaky hands. Tears fled from his eyes as he opened it up. He searched through the index until he found the page number and turned to the book of Ezra. Wiping his tears on his sleeve, he read.

Now in the first year of Cyrus king of Persia, that the word of the Lord by the mouth of Jeremiah might be fulfilled, the Lord stirred up the spirit of Cyrus king of Persia, that he made a proclamation throughout all his kingdom, and put it also in writing, saying…

The words came out through the lump in his throat. With a deep breath, he continued. The page blurred as his eyes filled. He blinked to keep them at bay.

"My son is Ezra. He's a good boy. Keep reading."

Ezra sucked in a breath and continued to read. *"Thus saith Cyrus, king of Persia, The Lord God of heaven hath given me all the kingdoms of the earth; and he hath charged me to build him a house at Jerusalem, which is in Judah."*

Soon a soft snore came from beside him, and he closed the book. Ezra stood and leaned over the broken man. He touched his worn face softly and then with sorrow, he turned to leave.

He rushed out of the room and back to the front of the building. He didn't care who saw how broken he was, he just needed fresh air and time to think.

"Sir," the nurse at the front desk called.

He turned around. "Yes?"

She slid a single key across the desk. On it was attached a plastic hospital band that said two words — Ezra McCain.

"What is this?"

"It's a key to a safe deposit box. I don't know what's inside, but your father gave explicit instructions when he… well before he was so far along in his disease, he said if you should come, to give it to you."

Ezra stared at the key as if it were a snake.

"Maybe it will help answer some questions?"

"Yeah, maybe. Thank you." Ezra took the key and held it in his hand. He walked out the door, staring at it, wondering.

How many years had it sat in a drawer somewhere waiting for him to show? And what would be in the box when he opened it? Did he even want to know?

Hoping it would give him some kind of closure, Ezra pushed the key into his pocket and headed out.

20

———

CHARLOTTE

Charlotte woke up with a start. Sitting up in bed, she looked out her window. It was still dark out. The clock on her bedside table said four a.m. Yawning, she scooted from her bed, got on her knees, and prayed. It was something she'd done for as long as she could remember.

Once she had finished and said an extra prayer for Ezra, she put on her robe and went downstairs to start the coffee. Nothing seemed to work without a potent dose of dark French roast.

Whispered voices in the living room stirred her curiosity. Peeking into the room, she saw Cole and Samantha cuddled up on the couch. Upset that Cole had broken the one rule she'd set for him, she walked in.

"You two are up early," she said.

Cole looked up startled. "Oh, hey sis. I thought you'd still be asleep."

"So, I see. Cole, could I talk to you for a moment in the kitchen?"

"Wait, no," Samantha stood. "It's not what you think. We were going to… I mean… well—" she looked at Cole.

"Might as well tell Miss Nosey Bottom now," he said.

"We wanted to get an early start on painting the store. It was supposed to be a surprise for you."

Charlotte's face fell. The two of them were wearing old, worn-out clothes perfect for painting.

When she didn't speak, Samantha came around to her. "Charlotte, I wouldn't disrespect your home like that. Nothing was going on. I was just telling him about…well, you'll have to wait and see, but I swear, it's completely innocent."

Cole came up beside her. "Seriously. Nothing's going on." He put his hands in the air. "We just wanted to get an early start."

"Okay, then." Ashamed of where her thoughts had gone, she smiled. "No harm done. Why don't we have some breakfast? I've got coffee brewing."

Relief showed in Samantha's eyes. "Yeah, sure. I make a mean omelet."

Together they made a quick breakfast as they chatted. Charlotte liked the girl more each time they spoke. Samantha had a wholesome way about her that made Charlotte believe she was the perfect girl for her brother. The thought that she'd almost had that same love with Ezra saddened her deeply. Where was he? Had he started that fire at the Monroe house? If he had, she didn't know if she could ever forgive him.

"Have you checked on Clementine?" Cole asked as they sat down to eat. "She should foal any day now."

"I'm going to check after breakfast. Then I'll come and help you two paint the store."

"Oh, no you don't. We got this. Samantha has it all planned out. We want it to be a surprise."

"You know how I hate surprises, Cole. And the guests will be here tomorrow."

"It won't take long. Don't worry, we'll get it done by the end of the day. You just keep your nose away from it. Sew up some more of those stuffed animals or something."

Charlotte took a bite of her eggs. "Fine, but if you two come out with more paint on you than the walls, I'm not going to be happy." Her words brought her back to her and Ezra installing the tile. *I'll give you a kiss for every tile you lay.* Her heart yearned for him to be back there on the ranch with her. *Ezra, what are you doing? Where are you?*

"You hear her, Sammy? No face painting allowed."

Samantha leaned in and kissed him on the cheek. "Walls only. I promise."

Cole's face turned a lovely shade of red as he grinned.

Feeling their flirting was a bit too much for her, Charlotte finished her breakfast and stood. "I'm going to check on Clementine."

The two lovebirds giggled and whispered some more, and Charlotte rolled her eyes. She couldn't blame her brother, though. She'd been just as happy in Ezra's arms. It was the only place she wanted to be.

Not even bothering to get dressed, she headed out to the stable. Clementine had been placed in a larger open area by herself to give her plenty of room to foal. Walking in that direction, she stopped to talk to each of the others. Their wounds were all healed, and it was time to test their emotional scars. She was hopeful that they were ready to carry riders once again, but planned to put them each through a series of tests to be sure they were ready to go.

As soon as she got to the back of the stable, Charlotte covered her mouth in awe. There, next to Clementine, stood a beautiful slick-skinned foal. Her mother was bathing her lovingly. She couldn't be more than an hour old.

Charlotte walked gently toward the mother and foal. "Hey, Clementine," she cooed. "I see you're a momma now. Good job, girl." She reached up and petted the mare. "How you feeling?"

Clementine nudged Charlotte with her nose.

"You did a good job, girl. She's nice and healthy."

Charlotte walked slowly to the foal, who stood behind her mother. "It's okay. Let me get a look at you."

The foal allowed her to come closer. Upon further inspection, she noted that there was another baby girl in the family. "What a pretty filly you are," she cooed.

Charlotte backed away and went to the area where she'd left the supplies needed to get the foal cleaned up and ready to nurse. With a soft, clean towel, she cleaned out the foal's nostrils and then, with a Betadine solution, she soaked the spot where the umbilical cord had already come away. "This will stop you from getting any infection."

She rubbed the foal down softly, desensitizing her ears, nose, and mouth. "What should we name you, girl?" she asked as the filly warmed up to her. "Doc Evans will be so happy to see you came on your own."

She directed the filly to her mother's teats, and she grabbed on easily and instinctually began to nurse. The bonding between mare and filly was important, and those two were already doing well. Clementine cleaned her young as she nursed.

"Lucky. I think we should call you, Lucky. After all, I thought for sure we'd lost you both."

Once she finished nursing, Charlotte led the two outside to the corral where they could bond more while she cleaned up the stable. One by one she led each horse outside as she did each morning. As they hit the corral, each horse came over to get a look at the newest member of the family. Titus played with the foal, nudging her in the bottom.

"Is that your foal, Titus?" Charlotte asked. Of course she was. He was the only stallion on the ranch. The rest were geldings, which made for calmer trail horses.

Clementine took immediate offense to his antics and nosed Titus away.

"Come on, Daddy, leave them alone." She led Titus away, then came back and brought Clementine and Lucky into a ringed off area of the corral. When it came to mothers, no matter whether human, horse or otherwise, they were always protective of their young.

Back in the main corral area, Charlotte ran the horses through a battery of tests. Leaving Samson and Clementine, there were seven horses to work, and each of them got an equal amount of her time. Cole was better at that sort of thing, but he and Samantha were being so secretive about painting walls that she decided not to bother them.

After spending the entire day running them through an extensive workout, testing their skittishness to surrounding noises and objects, she concluded that all of them but one, Titus, were ready for the trails. He was a wayward beast anyway, and they rarely used him for trail rides unless she or Cole rode him.

Checking her phone, she saw it was already late evening. She got the horses cleaned and brushed, then led them back to their stalls where she fed them. Heading back to the house, she planned to fall out on the couch and rest her weary body. Before she could make it there, she spotted Cole and Samantha sitting on the bench outside the store. They were engaged in a kiss.

She cleared her throat, and they looked up, blushing. "You're back. Hey, we finished up just in time, come in and look."

"I thought you promised to get more on the walls than each other?" She smirked. "Looks like that didn't work."

They looked down at their clothes. "Well, we had a little fun after the work was done. Come, look. I think you'll like it."

"What color did you paint the walls, anyway?" She was getting nervous seeing the variety of hues on their clothes and faces. "I thought we agreed on an off white."

Cole said nothing more as he led her into the store. As soon as she walked through the door, she was assaulted by the most beautiful sight she'd ever seen. A mural of a desert scene joined each of the walls. The longest of them held a set of mountains with the sun setting behind them in beautiful shades of reds and purples. Above was painted the words — *C&C Trails and Lodging.*

"It's… wow! It's amazing. I love it."

"Samantha did all the work. Isn't she a great artist?"

"Samantha! You did this? I mean, what am I saying, of course, Cole didn't do it."

Cole wrinkled his nose. "Wait a minute, now. See that cactus?" He pointed to a small, green stick off in the distance. "I painted that one."

"That's a cactus?" she teased, then looked at it closer. Not wanting to hurt his feelings, she said, "Oh, look. It sure is."

Cole and Samantha laughed. Samantha more than Cole.

"Do you like it?" Samantha asked shyly. "I mean, really. We can paint over it if you—"

"Are you crazy? This is gorgeous. I love it!" She hugged Samantha, thanking her for the gift. She looked around the room. "Now we just have to get the stuff back in here. I can't wait until our guests see it."

"We can do that tomorrow. Let's give the paint some time to dry, and the room needs to air out a bit," Samantha said. "By morning it should be ready to go."

They walked back to the house together, Charlotte still amazed at how everything was coming along.

"How's Clementine?" Cole asked.

"Oh! I forgot to tell you. She foaled. A nice little filly. I named her Lucky. She's perfectly healthy. Doc Evans will be here in the morning to give her a full check-up."

She'd have told him earlier but he and Samantha had insisted she stay away from the store while she was painting and then she got caught up in the rest of the horses and it had totally slipped her mind.

"Lucky, huh. I like it."

"Can we see her, Cole? I've never seen a newborn foal."

Cole smiled at her adoringly. "Of course, we'll go after dinner."

Ignoring their loving stares, Charlotte said. "I put the horses through all the tests Daddy taught us, I think they're ready to ride."

"I knew it wouldn't take much. They've been well-bred and taken care of. Samantha and I will take a few of them out on the trail in the morning, just to be sure. How many riders are coming?"

"A family of four."

"Good, we'll ride two out and let the other two straggle behind then switch them out on the way back." Cole cared for the horses just as much as she did. He would be sure to take every precaution to make sure they and their riders were safe.

"Sounds like a plan. I need to soak in a hot bath. You two can find something to eat."

"I think sandwiches will do," Cole answered. "We're all beat."

Samantha nodded her agreement, and Charlotte headed to her

bathroom to start a nice long bubble bath. Her body ached from head to toe. She'd gotten up so early and worked harder than she had in a long time.

As she removed her soiled clothes and slid into the hot water, she closed her eyes and let the water calm her aches. All except for the pain in her heart that nothing could not soften but seeing Ezra again and knowing he was safe.

21

————

EZRA

Ezra headed up to the Wells Fargo in town. There were several other banks in the area, but the small WF above the number fifteen on the wristband was an indication that it was a Wells Fargo key. At least his father had given him some kind of idea where to look.

Walking up to the bank, he didn't know what to expect. He didn't really care. After seeing his father, he needed no more explanation. He was a man withering away before his time, and Ezra had settled it in his heart to forgive him. He didn't excuse his father's actions. There was no way to do that. He had called out for him as if somewhere deep down in his deteriorating brain, he remembered him. That reading of the book of Ezra would bring him back, or at least soothe his mind. It made Ezra believe he was sorry for his actions. That was enough for him.

He went inside and walked to the front desk. Showing the bank teller the key and his ID, the man verified it in the system and led him back to a room filled with small safes. They inserted their keys, and the attendant left him to the room. On the far wall was a table with a couple of chairs. He brought the box to the table and sat down in front of it.

A nervousness fell over him, and he turned away from it. He wasn't sure he was ready for what he would find inside. He needed to get back to Charlotte. She'd probably thought he abandoned her and he was missing her like crazy. Eager to get it over with, he reached inside and pulled out a small white envelope. On the outside, written in his father's handwriting, was one word, Ezra.

His hands shook as he opened the envelope and pulled out a piece of lined paper. He read the short message.

SON,

I am sorry for what I have done to you. Your wounds are deep, and I am the cause. I don't deserve your forgiveness, so I won't ask for it. Inside this box is an envelope with $210,000 and the paperwork for the selling of the house. With my care completely taken care of, every penny goes to you.

I don't presume to buy your love. What is destroyed can never be purchased with money. I just hope that you will use the money well.

THE WORDS SOUNDED SO MUCH like his father. Short and to the point. It was almost as if he could hear it coming straight from his lips. He set the letter aside before he finished. He needed a break from his father's words.

Ezra checked the bottom of the box to find an envelope full of money. He opened it up, and a car key fell out of it. He looked at it for a moment, turning it around in his hand. Under the envelope was a certified letter along with the paperwork from the sale of the house. He stared at the paperwork for a long time before taking his eyes off of it. His father had sold the house and given him the money. He picked the note back up.

IN THE BOX is also a key to my old Chevy. Maybe you don't want it. If you don't, that's okay. You can sell it. It's at Larry's house. He promised to keep it in good repair for you.

I am being transferred to a facility soon. But I've done this to myself. They call it some silly disease, but I think I have drunk myself into forgetting the harm that I've caused. It's easier that way. I've always been one to take the easy way out.

Enough said. Take care of yourself, son. You have had to do it all your life. I know you will continue.

Love,
Your Father

EZRA TOOK a deep breath to stave off the tears itching to break free. At less than fifty-years-old, his father had wasted away to nothing but a shell of a man. Whether or not it was Alzheimer's, he didn't believe his father was willing to come out of his walking coma. He thought about what the old vet had told him. *The past ain't a straightforward thing to recover from.* His father had suffered plenty. It was time to give it a rest.

He went back up to the front of the bank and handed over the key. With the money, certified letter, and sales documentation, he opened a bank account, keeping a small amount out for his immediate needs.

Thirty minutes later, Ezra walked out of the bank with a temporary bank card, the letter from his father, and a key to his father's old car.

In another half an hour, he stood at the door of his father's old friend's house. Larry. He hadn't seen him since he was a young boy. He knocked on the door hesitantly, not sure he wanted to see him.

"Can I help you?" Larry asked from behind a security door.

"Hi, Larry. My father… uh… he asked me to stop by."

Larry stared at him curiously. "Your father? Who would that be?"

Ezra's instinct was to turn and leave, but his feet wouldn't move. "William McCain."

Larry's eyes signaled recognition. "Ezra? Little Ezra?"

The next thing he knew, the door swung open, and Larry's arms flew around him. "Little Ezra McCain. My, you've sure grown. Come on in. Come on in."

Ezra followed him in.

"So, you came back to see him, huh? I sure am sorry for what happened. Your father and I went out looking for you after you left. He was a mess. He's never been the same since."

Ezra didn't know what to say to that. He'd have never thought his father had even cared that he'd left. His throat itched. "He came looking for me?"

Larry's eyes sobered. "Ezra, I can't be sorrier for what he did to you. The day you left." He looked away, his eyes showing pain. "He told me what he did. What he'd been doing. He was a very sick man, and he took it out on you."

"It's in the past. I'm over it."

"No. don't go writing this off as nothing. Your father told me that if you ever came back, to tell you that you're not to blame. When he lost your mother, his mind snapped. That's no excuse for taking it out on you. I'm not defending him. I just want you to understand that your father loved you. He just didn't know how…" Larry shifted on his feet. "No, I'm not going to go there. He was wrong, plain, and simple. I can't tell you how sorry I am that I didn't know about what was happening to you. I could have… should have helped."

"Can I take a look at the car?" Ezra wanted to get away from that line of discussion. The past was the past, and he would deal with it in his own time, but rehashing it was doing nothing but making him frustrated.

"Yeah, sure. It's in the garage. I've kept the maintenance up on it, and I take it out to drive every Sunday. It's all yours."

Ezra followed Larry through the house and to the back door that led to the garage. As soon as he saw it, his hands shook. He shoved them into his pockets.

"Suspended from school?" His father grabbed him by the ear, dragging him to the very same car. "I'll teach you a lesson."

Blocking any more thoughts from his head, he looked away. When would he ever be able to see the past as anything but painful? He could sell it, and maybe that was a good idea, but it was the only thing he had from his past. It not only represented the bad, but the good times he'd had before his mother passed away. Those were all now a blur, shut out by her prolonged agony.

God, help me figure this all out.

"You thinking of selling it? I'd buy it from you if you were."

Immediately his decision was made. "No. I think I'll keep it."

"Good. Your father would be… I'm glad you're keeping it. You have the key." Larry hit the button for the automatic garage door opener and then pulled the spare from his keyring and handed it to him. "It's gassed up and ready to go. The title's in the glove box. It's been signed over to you. Just take it to the MVD, and you're all set."

Ezra walked to the car and opened the door. He sat down inside, feeling the soft leather seats with the palm of his hand. His father had loved the car more than his own son. Refusing to allow his mind to go that route again, he waved to Larry and put the key in the ignition. Backing out, he looked back to see a sad expression on Larry's face. He had tried to talk to him, but there was just not too many things to say. All of them brought up painful memories he'd rather not deal with.

The older car drove as smoothly as if he'd bought it off a new car lot. Larry had taken good care of it. Ezra was ready to get back to Charlotte, but first, he had a couple of stops to make.

Pulling up into the parking lot of the nursing home he'd been at merely hours before, Ezra had some things to say to his father. Whether or not he understood them was of no consequence. They needed to be said.

He parked the car and went inside.

"Mr. McCain, you're back so soon."

"Yes. I'd like to speak to my father again if that's okay."

The woman looked up to a clock on the side wall. "Sure. Visiting hours are over in thirty minutes."

Ezra nodded, and she picked up the phone to call him an escort back. A moment later, the same woman who had brought him in the first time poked her head out. "Look who's back. Your father has been talking about you since you left."

Most likely his father was talking about the Bible book and not him, but he took it with kindness, anyway. "Thanks. I just need a moment with him, and then I'll be out of your hair."

As he followed her back, she rattled on about what a good mood senior Mr. McCain had been in ever since their visit. Ezra didn't quite get it. His father was completely out of his mind. How they could tell he was in a better or worse mood was beyond him.

He entered the room. His father sat on a couch with a book in his lap. He looked up and smiled at them as if he actually saw them.

"Guess who came back to see you, Mr. McCain. It's your son, Ezra."

"Ezra. I'm reading the book of Ezra. He was a scribe, you know." His father patted the book in his lap.

The nurse smiled and patted his shoulder. "He's no more cognitive, but I think inside, he's found a bit of peace. I believe your visit was the cause."

"Thanks. Could I have a moment with him alone?"

"Sure. I'll be down the hall if you need me."

The nurse left, and Ezra sat down next to his father. "Hey, Dad. How are you doing?"

"I had a son once. His name was Ezra."

"Yeah. I heard." There was no use arguing. "I just wanted to tell you I forgive you, Dad. I know you don't understand me right now, but when Mom passed away, I was—"

"Yes, Victoria. She was a beauty, wasn't she? Love of my life. Every time I looked into the boy's eyes, I saw her."

"I know. And it hurt you."

"No. No. I hurt him. My poor Ezra. He was a good boy, and I ran him off."

"Ezra forgives you."

"You know my son?" His father stared into his eyes and Ezra could have sworn he saw a glimmer of recognition.

"I do. He wants you to know, he's okay. And he forgives you."

"I love the book of Ezra. I read it every day."

Ezra patted his father's hand and stood. There was no way to know if his father understood what he was saying, but he felt that a weight had been lifted in speaking the words.

"Dad, I . . . I'll come back and visit again. You take care of yourself, okay?" He wasn't ready to say the words *I love you*, but he felt in his heart that he could someday say them and mean it. For now, he could only make the promise of returning.

His father's eyes glossed over, and he stared out the window. A smile stood on his face, and Ezra wasn't sure what it meant, but if it gave him a small amount of comfort, he was happy for it.

Ezra left the nursing home, his heart a little lighter. He had one more stop to make before heading back to the ranch and begging Charlotte to forgive him for leaving in the dead of night without warning. At the first fast-food restaurant he found, he turned in and headed through the drive-thru.

"Can I get forty hamburgers, please? And throw in twenty medium fries."

"Sir, did you say forty?"

"Yes, ma'am. And twenty medium fries."

Twenty minutes later, he was on his way to the underpass. Parking his car in the dirt, he grabbed the bags and headed up to the several homeless people that gathered around. He'd been there. He knew just how far a couple of hamburgers would go to lighten their loads. Passing out several burgers, he sat on the ground next to the old vet and ate with them. He was no longer homeless. Even if Charlotte rejected him for leaving, he had enough money to get his life started, even so, he had a heart for the people who struggled every day just for a bite to eat.

"Looks like things went well," Stanley said.

"Thank you for talking to me. You gave me much food for thought. I think I'm in a much better state of mind now."

"Weren't me, young man. That there's the power of God."

"Yeah. I've got some more things to figure out, but I'll be back. Thanks again."

Ezra took his last bite of burger, shoved a couple of fries in his mouth and said his goodbyes. The next stop would be the hardest.

22

CHARLOTTE

Charlotte sat at the kitchen table going through the monthly bills. She sorted them into priority. The ones that were overdue, she placed on top. With the additional income, she could pay a good portion of them up to date and no longer felt that overwhelming feeling she was about to drown in a sea of bills. The ranch wasn't exactly on the plus side yet, but they were surviving. That was more than she could say the month prior, and she had hoped it would get better.

Two of her rooms were currently filled. One with a family of three, and the other a single gentleman who spent most of his time on his computer in his room. Another family was due in soon, and she anticipated having a full house. She'd made baked goods all morning, and Cole had gone out and bought the fixings for a light lunch. She was not under obligation to feed them a dinner meal, but with no restaurants within miles, she decided to put on a large pot of spaghetti.

Her dream was to turn part of the store into a restaurant where she could entertain guests completely. For now, that would have to wait. They were barely getting by as it was.

The sound of a vehicle pulling up alerted her that her guests were there. She went out the door and waved at the family as their car parked in the driveway. A man got out, waving back as his wife went to the back to unbuckle the cutest little girl sitting in a toddler seat. He walked up to her, his family not far behind.

"Hi. My name's Jacob," he said. "This is my wife, Katherine, and my daughter Emily." They sidled up next to him and smiled.

"It's so nice to meet you. I have your room ready." After the first people had stayed and she realized the rooms had not contained a smaller bed for the children, she and Cole had gotten together some bunk frames, and she'd made a thin cotton mattress to go on top. They were probably not the most comfortable, but Cole had short-ened the legs, so they fit underneath the bigger beds. One day, she'd have all the comforts of home for them, but for now, she'd just have to make due.

She showed them to their room.

"This is so cute!" Katherine said. "Look, Emmie. There's a special bed for you."

The sweet little girl put her hands to her face in a surprised smile. She couldn't have been more than three.

"The itinerary for the day is here." Charlotte picked up the paper she'd printed out. "We have another family staying with us and another young man. The other family has a ten-year-old boy who is excited to see the farm area of the ranch. We have a couple of chickens and an old milking cow that loves affection. We also have a foal who was born only a couple of days ago. She loves the attention too. I'd love for you to join us if you care to."

"That would be great!" the mother said. "Emmie, you want to see a moo cow?"

"I love moo cows!"

The father was already pulling out his laptop. "You two go. I'll just catch up on some work."

Katherine gave Charlotte a strained look. "Sorry. He's a workaholic."

"I heard that."

"It's okay. Maybe he'd prefer to join us on the trail ride later."

Jacob grunted, already into his own thoughts.

Katherine rolled her eyes. "Come on, Emmie, let's go see the moo-cow and chickens."

Emily headed for the door. "Bye, Daddy," she called.

Once outside the door, Katherine sighed. "I can't ever get that man to take a second away from his work. I thought this little trip would help."

"Understandable. Maybe we can get him out of his shell later." She smiled but felt bad for the woman.

The other family came from their room.

"Katherine, this is Jonathan and Tia. And their son, Jon Jr."

Katherine shook hands and introduced her daughter.

"Can we see the cow now?" Jon Jr. asked. "I've been waiting all day."

Charlotte grinned. It was only nine o'clock in the morning. He couldn't have been out of bed for more than an hour or two. "Let's do it."

Cole walked up with Samantha behind him, and Charlotte made more introductions.

"Anyone ready to milk the cow?" he asked. Cole was great with kids. One day, he'd be a father just like theirs was. Attentive and protective. It saddened her that Jacob sat in his room in front of his laptop while his daughter had her first experience with a real moo-cow.

"Someone say cow milking?" the handsome loner asked, standing in his doorway. "I'm writing this book about a farm. The best experience is in doing, right?"

"Absolutely." Cole shook his hand. "Cole."

"Thomas. Let's do this." Thomas looked in Charlotte's direction with a wink.

Her face reddened at the attention. He was a tall man with light-brown hair and the bluest eyes she'd ever seen. Handsome, for sure, but nothing could hold a candle to Ezra. Her heart beat heavily at the thought of him. If only she knew he was safe.

Once they had all pet the cow and helped gather eggs with chickens pecking at their feet, Charlotte asked if they would like to visit their foal, Lucky.

The kids were all in. As she led them to the stables, she watched the young girl holding her mother's hand excitedly. Her heart yearned for a child of her own.

They found Lucky nursing on her mother at the back of the stable, and she went inside, waited for her to finish, then led Lucky to the fence that separated her from the kids. Clementine followed protectively behind. Charlotte rubbed Clementine's muzzle, letting her know it was okay.

The kids reached through the bars and gently petted the foal.

"I want a horsey, Mommy," Emily said. "She's so soft and pretty."

Jon Jr. agreed readily. "Me, too. Daddy, can we buy Lucky?"

"Lucky is not for sale," Charlotte interrupted. "Sorry about that."

She'd given up so much already. There was no way she wanted to sell even one more horse.

"Aw, no fair," Jon Jr. said but shrugged shyly when his father gave him a reprimanding stare. "Sorry."

CHARLOTTE WAS TIRED. They'd spent the entire day showing the families around the ranch, milking cows, pointing out the desert plants, and finally taking them on a trail ride. Of course, Jacob had declined everything, saying he had work to do. Charlotte was almost tempted to pull the plug on the router for the Wi-Fi just to make him come out and join his wife, but in the end, she decided it was better to allow his wife to deal with him.

They'd all had their share of spaghetti and thanked her profusely. She'd gotten tips from all of them and was happy to add that to the jar that helped to keep the electricity running. All in all, it was a good day.

"Can we make cactus candy now?" Jon Jr. asked, wiping leftover spaghetti sauce from his chin.

"Let's save that for tomorrow," his father chided. "It's been a long day."

"Cole is getting a fire set up in the back if you'd like to relax. I'd love to keep Jon with me and make some candy." She was exhausted, but soon it would be bedtime, and she'd get rest. She needed to make their stay enjoyable.

"Can I, Dad?"

"I'll stay with him, you go relax by the fire with the guys," Tia said.

Katherine agreed to stay with Emily and make candy as well. They got together at the table, and Charlotte brought out the supplies. As she set them down, a shadow entered the doorway. She looked up, and her body froze.

"Um, excuse me for a moment. I'll be right back."

All eyes turned to Ezra standing in the doorway. She rushed to the door, pushed past him and out to the back of the store. All the worry that had built up inside of her had come out like a typhoon ready to hit.

"Charlotte, wait. Where are you going?"

She kept her pace without turning back to him. Once she reached the fire pit, she headed for Samantha who was sitting next to Cole. The fire was already blazing. Leaning down, she whispered into Samantha's ear asking her to take over the cactus candy making for her.

Samantha gave her a strange look. "I don't know how to make it. Is something —" Her eyes caught on Ezra's. "Oh, yeah, sure. I think we can muddle along."

"There's a recipe on the table." Charlotte's insides shook as she looked back to Ezra.

"Sure, no problem."

Cole looked up and as soon as his eyes met Ezra's, he stood. "Excuse me," Cole said and headed toward Ezra.

"Cole, wait." Charlotte put a hand on his chest. "Let me talk to him."

"He burned down—"

"Tend to the guests, please. Let me talk to him. There's no use getting everyone upset."

Cole stepped back. Narrowing his eyes at Ezra for a moment, he looked away and went back to the guests. Charlotte turned and stormed off toward the stable. Ezra followed.

"What's going on?" he called. "I'm sorry I left without telling you, but I had some things—"

Charlotte spun around so quickly, she nearly fell. "Left without telling me? You think that's it?" She spun back around and continued walking.

"Charlotte, would you just stop? Talk to me?"

Turning again, she said, "You could have killed someone!"

23

———

EZRA

"What are you talking about?" Ezra watched her face. "Killed who?"

"The Monroe fire. I thought we agreed you wouldn't go after him."

His heart fell into his chest. He'd forgotten all about his first intention and how it must look when he left so abruptly. "Charlotte, I didn't start any fire, I swear."

"No?" She looked for a second like she wanted to believe him.

"Wait, there was a fire at Garrett's house?"

That fire came back into her eyes. "Please, just tell me the truth. I can't handle—"

"I didn't do it. I swear!" Ezra raised his hands.

"Oh, yeah?" Her hands went to her hips. "Then why is our gas can and all the gas from the truck missing?"

Ezra lowered his head. He should have known she would think that. So much had happened since then that he hadn't even thought about what it must look like to her. But then again, he hadn't known that the house had actually burned down either. Who else would want to hurt Garrett?

132

"Come with me." He continued to walk toward the stable, only this time he was leading, and she wasn't moving.

"I'm not going anywhere with you until you explain."

He turned to face her. "What I have to show you will explain everything."

Hesitantly, she followed him. When they got to the back of the stables, he showed her the missing gas can. "Lift it."

She picked up the gas can and sniffed it. "It's still full of fuel. But why, then?"

Ezra sat on the ground and leaned his head against the back of the stable. "I planned to. I was so angry after I heard you and the doc talking. He said I was dangerous to your family every day I stayed here. I wanted to put a stop to all of this."

"Ezra, he didn't mean—" She sat next to him.

"Yes, he did. And he was right. I don't blame him. But that night, I was so consumed with anger that I got the stuff together, and I planned on burning down his house."

"But you didn't?"

"No. I walked all the way over there, and I was set to do it. But when I watched through the window for a while as they were talking, I thought about the reason I left in the first place. I'm not a killer, Charlotte. Wanting revenge and taking it are two different things."

"You're right. I'm glad you didn't do it."

"You believe me?"

"Of course, I do. Ezra, I have been praying for you all this time. I asked God to change your heart. Only, I thought—"

"You thought it was too late for me. That I'd already gone too far."

Charlotte nodded. "Yes. I'm sorry for not believing in you."

"I don't blame you. The evidence was all right there. I would've thought the same thing. I planned to do it, but the more I listened to them talk, the more I realized that Garrett wasn't the reason I was so angry. It was my father I was angry with, not Garrett. Wait. Is Garrett okay? What about the others?"

"The police came here the next morning. They said no one was in the house when the fire started."

Ezra let out a deep sigh. Whether Garrett was a bad man or not was irrelevant. The thought of the man who raised him burning to death was unsettling.

"Where did you go then? You've been gone for days."

"So, I came back, left the gas can here, and went to confront him. My father, I mean." He wasn't ready to tell her about the money he'd inherited. He didn't want her thinking he could buy her love. He would earn it, and when he told her, it would be theirs. At least that was his hope.

"You did? What happened?"

"He's nothing but a shell. He doesn't even know who I am."

"Oh, Ezra. I'm so sorry."

"It's better that way. I was so enraged at him that I might have done something stupid. But while I was in town, I met this man. He was a vet who lived on the streets. A good guy, he——" Suddenly he felt embarrassed about his new-found belief. Not ashamed of God, but worried that she might find it all too contrived. Like he'd say anything to get her back.

"He what?"

"He told me about God. Charlotte, I know you think——"

"That's great, Ezra. I've been telling you all along. At least trying to."

"I know you have. But it was… he made so much sense."

"I'm glad." Charlotte touched his hand.

"Charlotte, I'm so in love with you. I can't imagine my life without you."

Charlotte stared at him for a long time. "Ezra, I——"

At her hesitation, he placed a finger over her lips. "You don't have to say anything. Just know that I care about you. I'm going to get my life together and prove to you, and God, and whoever else, that I am worthy."

"God already knows," she whispered. "Everything happens for a reason."

"I believe that, Charlotte. But how do I right the wrongs I've done?"

"It will all work out in the end."

"How? There are so many people I stole from. I just don't know where or how to——"

"Ezra, you were so young. You did what Garrett told you to do. If you asked God to forgive you, then He has."

"But people —— how do they forgive me? I don't even know who I stole from. All my life, Garrett has told me that what we were doing was okay because they had so much and we had nothing. But it wasn't right. Those people worked hard and earned what they had . . . and . . . and we took from them." He felt like a young child again. Lost and confused.

"I don't know the answer. I only know that if you trust in Him, He will make it better."

But would God give him his heart's desire? Charlotte? He was willing to suffer the consequences of his actions, but he didn't want to lose her.

"Come on, let's talk to Cole. He's pretty upset about all of this." She stood and held out a hand to him.

"He's not going to believe me."

"Not right away. Give him some time."

Ezra didn't know if all the time in the world would change the way Cole felt about him and that mattered to him. But trust didn't come easy. Taking her hand, he stood, and they headed to the lodging rooms.

Cole sat by the fire chatting when they got there. His glare told Ezra it would be no simple task to win him over. Ezra's mind continued to go back to Garrett's place. Who had set it on fire? How would he clear his name with Cole or anyone else? Did the police suspect him?

Cole stood and walked around the corner out of hearing of the guests.

"You shouldn't be here." Cole stared at him in defiance. "You've caused enough trouble."

"Cole, he didn't do it."

Cole looked up at his sister. "Don't let love blind you. The evidence is all there."

24

CHARLOTTE

Charlotte looked back to the lodging rooms. "Let's go in the house. We don't need to disturb our guests." She knew her brother. He wasn't yelling yet, but whenever he wanted to make a point, he tended to get loud.

Cole gave Ezra another glare and stormed off toward the house.

"This is too much. Maybe I should leave," Ezra said. "I've caused enough trouble."

"Maybe I should talk to him alone. It's late, and you've had a rough couple of days. Why don't you take a shower and get some sleep?"

"I should talk to him. All this trouble is because of me."

There was no way Cole would calm down enough to listen unless she spoke to him alone, showed him the evidence, and explained to him what happened. Ezra's presence would only provoke him more.

"Let me talk to him tonight. I know my brother. He'll be reasonable, but I should do it alone."

Ezra shook his head. "I'm sorry for all the trouble I've caused." He kissed her forehead and turned to leave.

Charlotte wanted to call him back and tell him none of this was his fault, but she didn't. They'd lived a quiet existence before he came along. Convincing Cole of his innocence would not be easy. Their entire life depended on keeping the ranch up and going. That couldn't happen if trouble followed them around every corner. For the first time, Charlotte understood why Ezra had been so set on leaving. Without even trying, he was causing problems. Until he could break away from the hold Garrett had on him, his life would never be normal.

Charlotte watched him go into his room. A sadness came over her. The situation was too big to handle on her own. Even if she convinced Cole that Ezra didn't start the fire, which she truly believed was the truth, how would she convince him that Ezra was not a danger to the ranch?

Charlotte went back to their guests, who were still sitting by the fire. The kids had returned to their parents and everyone looked exhausted. Soon they were up and heading to their rooms.

"Thanks for a wonderful time." The mother touched her arm. "You have really made us feel at home."

"It was my pleasure. Have a good night," Charlotte said.

She picked up the shovel as her guests closed their doors and piled dirt onto the fire. Once it was completely out, she headed back to the house.

"Hey," Samantha called from behind. "Can I talk to you for a minute?"

She turned to see Samantha standing just outside her door. She was wearing a light-blue pajama shorts set.

"Hi, Samantha. I thought you were down for the night."

"I was. Well, I was reading, anyway. I heard you two outside."

"Why don't we go inside the store. I don't want to disturb our guests."

Samantha nodded and followed her to the store. Charlotte unlocked the door and went inside. Samantha followed.

"What's on your mind?" Charlotte asked.

"I know you know your brother better than anyone else, but he talks to me, so… well, I thought maybe I could tell you how he's feeling about all of this."

"I know what he thinks. He thinks Ezra is dangerous, and it doesn't matter that he makes me happy."

"That's not true. Well, some of it is. I mean, if Ezra started that fire at Monroe's house, then yes, we both believe he's dangerous."

"He didn't."

Samantha watched her for a moment. "You're sure?"

"Yes. He said he didn't, and he showed me the proof." Charlotte told Samantha what Ezra had shared with her. She explained to her about the full container of fuel that had gone unused. "Ezra spent that time with his father."

"If all of that is true, then that's good news." Samantha stared out the window. Charlotte got the idea that she didn't believe a word of it. "Are you sure you're thinking with your head and not your heart?"

Heat warmed Charlotte's neck. "Of course, I believe him. Why would he lie? The gas tank was right there. He showed it to me. Ezra is not a killer." But an inkling of doubt sunk into her chest, warning her that maybe her heart was too close to the situation to reason. Not sure if she was trying to convince Samantha or herself, she said, "He's not lying."

"I hope you're right."

25

———

EZRA

Ezra sat up straight in his bed as the door to his room jiggled. Before his brain could understand what was happening, the door clicked and opened. He skittered to his feet as two men entered the room fully clothed in black from their shoes to the ski masks that hid their faces. They didn't need to remove their disguises. He knew who they were.

"What do you want?" He stepped back to the wall, tripping over his own boots.

"Boss wants to see you."

"I don't work for you… him … anymore."

"That why you burned down the house?"

"I had nothing to do with that." His insides shrunk in fear. Garrett would kill him if that's what he thought.

"Yeah, right. You can tell it to his face." Rhett stepped closer, grabbed his boots, and threw them at his feet. "Put em on."

"I'm not going anywhere with you." Ezra stared down at his boots.

"Yeah, you are." Bart pulled out his gun and pointed it in his face. "Tie him up."

Rhett pulled a roll of duct tape from his pocket and proceeded toward Ezra.

"Okay." Ezra placed his hands in the air. "I'll go." He reached down for his boots but stumbled backward when a blow hit him in the face. Rhett pulled his hand back and grabbed it with the other. "That's for the horse that kicked me in the face. Next one'll be for that punk kid who shot my leg out."

Not wanting to stir up any more anger with them, he put his hands in the air. "Please. I'll go, just leave the rest of them alone."

Rhett chuckled. "Oh, you'll go alright. Put your boots on."

"It's lucky for you, Garrett said to take you quietly, or every inch of this place would burn to the ground," he snarled. "Including your sweet Charlotte."

Ezra shook violently as he put on his boots. He had no plans to push them. One false move and they would disregard Garretts orders and have the whole place ablaze.

"Tie him up," Bart said. "He ain't getting away this time."

Before he could protest, Rhett pulled off a strip of tape and slapped it over his mouth. Ezra put up no struggle as the men taped his hands behind his back, then pushed him toward the door. "You got some walking to do, but don't think of running. I'll shoot you in the back myself."

Ezra walked out the door. Both men came up beside him, and each took an elbow. He saw no sign of their vehicle. They walked him off the property. About a half mile down the road, Ezra saw the outline of a truck. They were smart not to pull up into the drive like they'd done the first time.

They can do whatever they want to me. Please protect Charlotte.

Whatever the outcome, Ezra knew the end was near. Bart pulled down the tailgate and pushed Ezra toward the truck. "Get in."

Pain shot through his shoulder and up his neck as he tried to maneuver his way into the bed of the truck with his hands firmly taped behind his back. The guys laughed at his awkwardness as he struggled inside. As soon as he was in and sitting, Rhett taped his legs together.

"Don't think of going nowhere. I'll have a gun pointed on you the entire time. One fast move and we'll be cleaning your brains from the back of the truck."

Ezra nodded in agreement, but inside he wondered if getting his brains blown off would be better than whatever Garrett had planned for him. The will to live overcame him as Rhett and Bart jumped in the cab and spun off. His only chance of survival was if Garrett believed he didn't start the fire.

Questions spun through his head as to who had started the fire. The only logical conclusion he could come to was that Bart and Rhett had started it knowing Garrett would blame him. He'd told them he was dead, but the looks on their faces that night while Ezra stared through the window led him to believe they knew Garrett was lying. They were angry and wanted revenge. He wouldn't put it past them to burn down the house and then blame it on him. But there was no way to prove it.

Fifteen minutes later, the truck pulled into Garrett's long, dirt driveway. The house was burned to the ground. Not a single beam was standing. The charred remains of Garrett's entire life hit Ezra like a bullet to the chest. Nothing had survived.

The men came around the back, Rhett opened the tailgate, and Bart grabbed his shoulder by the shirt. The two of them dragged him out of the truck bed and down the dirt driveway that led to the only remaining building standing. An old stable that Garrett used to store stolen goods.

Opening the door, they tossed him inside, closed it and locked it. Ezra looked around the dark room. Goods were piled all around him. Things that had been stolen and were awaiting a safe time to sell them.

Garrett had taught him when he was young that it was best to let things lie low before reselling them. It was how they avoided arrest for so long. Once the owners had gotten their insurance money back and were no longer looking for the items, they took them to various dealers who were just as shady as they were.

Where was Garrett? Where were they going? The pain in Ezra's shoulder was unbearable, and his face felt like a truck had overrun it. It wore him down, but he had to stay awake. He could not allow

Garrett to catch him sleeping. It would show weakness, and Garrett would kill him before he had time to speak.

Instead of allowing the weariness to take him, Ezra spent his time petitioning God for Charlotte's safety. Nothing mattered to him more than being sure she was safe in all of this. His resolve was weakening that he could convince Garrett of the truth, so instead, he would do whatever it took to keep Charlotte safe. Even if it meant his own death.

26

CHARLOTTE

The sound of pounding awoke Charlotte from a deep sleep.

"Charlotte, open up!"

It was Cole. Charlotte jumped out of bed and rushed to the door. "What's going on?"

Samantha stood next to Cole wearing the same light-blue pajama set she'd worn when they'd spoken earlier.

"It's Ezra. They took him," Samantha cried.

"What do you mean? Who?"

"I don't know. I heard a commotion through the wall that connects our rooms. And then they were dragging him out at gunpoint, his mouth and hands taped."

"Who was it?" Charlotte shook as if she were standing in the arctic tundra.

"I don't know. They were wearing all black and had on masks."

"I think it was Garrett's men," Cole said.

Charlotte hadn't had the chance to talk to Cole about Ezra's innocence. By the time she got back to the house, he'd already been in bed. "Cole, he didn't do it. He didn't burn down Garrett's house."

"Samantha told me. I went out and saw the container still full of gasoline."

"You believe me, then?"

Cole nodded. "What are we going to do?"

"We have to help him. Garrett will surely kill him this time."

"We better call the police."

He was right. It was the only thing to do. There was no way they could go running over there, playing heroes. They'd all get killed. But if they involved the police, what would happen to Ezra? The words he'd said about wanting to face the consequences of his actions flowed through her head. Even if it caused Ezra problems with the police, at least he'd be alive.

"Call them. I'll get dressed."

Cole nodded and pulled out his phone. "We'll be downstairs."

Over an hour later, the same deputy who had come asking questions about the fire was knocking on their door.

"Come in." Charlotte waved for him to come inside.

Samantha explained how Ezra was taken from his room, and the officer asked a dozen questions before calling in backup.

"So, you're sure these men were from the Monroe property? What exactly would they have against this uh—" He glanced down at his notes. "Ezra McCain?"

Charlotte's insides fought over how much to tell him. Within seconds, the safety of Ezra won out, and she told him about Ezra being raised in a life of crime by Garrett. Maybe it would be worse on him, possibly it would get him arrested and thrown in jail, but she had to take a chance. It was the only way to convince the officer of the urgency of the matter.

Charlotte blurted out everything Ezra had told her about his life with Garrett Monroe. Cole stared at her, stunned. It was his first time hearing all that she had learned. She just hoped that it would change his view on Ezra. That it would help him understand, and the police, that Ezra was a victim in all of this. No matter what Ezra said, she believed he'd done those things out of necessity and had been forced into them by Garrett.

It was after dawn before the deputy called for backup and go out to the Monroe place. As soon as they left, Charlotte went to her knees and prayed for Ezra.

27

EZRA

Ezra lay on the ground, still bound and in complete darkness. Hours had passed, and he was weary. His wrists burned as the tape dug into his flesh. His hands tingled with the lack of blood flow reaching them. Each struggle to release himself from his bindings only made the pain unbearable.

The darkness of the room only intensified his urge to close his eyes, yet he'd not had an ounce of sleep. He spent the entire time praying for Charlotte's safety. That Garrett had not shown up yet worried Ezra that Garrett had gone to her place to do the unthinkable. He prayed it wasn't so. It would be stupid of Garrett to cause himself more problems by trying to harm Charlotte and her family, but if he wasn't there, where was he?

The door to the shed opened, and Ezra looked up. His eyes were tired, but there was no mistaking the man who stood before him. Garrett walked toward him. The look in his eyes was one of remorse. As if he was going to have to do something that upset him. At that moment, Ezra knew his life was over.

Garrett pulled a bucket over in front of Ezra. Turning it upside down, he sat on it. He stared at Ezra for a long time. "Do I even want to hear what you have to say?" he asked.

Ezra nodded. The fear inside him that Garrett would refuse to let him speak and pull his gun out was overwhelming. He breathed in a deep breath through his nose.

Garrett reached over and ripped off the tape from his mouth. "You have two minutes to tell me why I shouldn't put a bullet in your head."

Ezra's voice caught in his throat. He'd spent so much time praying that he hadn't thought of what he would say to Garrett. "I didn't burn down your house," he answered.

Garrett chuckled. "No? Hm, I suppose it was a lightning bug?"

"Garrett, you have to believe me. It wasn't me." As soon as the words were out of his mouth, a feeling came over him, and he decided to tell the entire truth. "I wanted to. After Rhett and Bart went over there and harassed Charlotte, I was so angry. I got the stuff together and came here. I thought you were still in jail. But I didn't do it. Instead, I listened to you tell those idiots that I was dead. That you had shot me between the eyes and buried me."

"Oh, you did, did you? Then you know that I tried everything in my power to stop from having to kill you. And then you went and burned down my house? And you think I should just let that slide?"

"I didn't do it. I swear."

Garrett stood so quickly the bucket fell backward. He grabbed his gun from his belt and swung it, hitting Ezra in the face. His jaw popped unnaturally as pain surged through his face.

"You think I'm stupid?" Spittle flew from Garrett's mouth as his face turned a beet-red. "You think I'm just supposed to believe you? After all I've done for you, and now you're going to look me in the face and lie?"

Ezra held his head low to ward off another blow to his face. The sound of the gun cocking made him look up. Garrett's gun was pointed right at his scalp. Ezra said a silent prayer.

"Put your hands up!" A voice called from the doorway.

Garrett turned around and shot at the intruder. The bullet hit the officer right in the head, and he dropped to the ground. Four more officers were behind him, and before Garrett could get off another shot, they had him straddled on the ground and were hand-cuffing him.

An officer came to him and cut away the tape from his arms and legs. As the officer arrested Garrett, he spouted off all kinds of crimes that the two of them had committed together.

"He's a common thief! And he burned down my house!" Garrett yelled as they dragged him out of the barn.

"Are you okay?" one officer asked. "It looks like your jaw is broken."

Ezra nodded. It was too painful to speak.

"There's an ambulance on the way to take you to the hospital, but then we will need to bring you in for questioning."

Ezra turned away as another officer covered the body of the dead officer. The smell of blood made him want to vomit. His body shook with the realization that the man had saved his life by taking the bullet that had been meant for him. Trying to put the image from his mind, he turned back to the officer and nodded.

He'd prayed that God would show him how he could make amends for all he had done, and he guessed this was what God had planned. The courts would decide whether he would pay for his crimes. It was okay. He'd admit to everything he'd done. He deserved whatever sentence they met out.

The ambulance came, and Ezra was taken to the hospital. After X-rays and exams, they found his jaw was not broken but only badly bruised.

"This a gunshot wound?" the doctor asked, inspecting his shoulder.

Ezra nodded. Before he could try to get a word out, he heard Charlotte on the other side of the curtain.

"I'm here to see Ezra."

The sound of her voice made him sigh with relief. She was okay.

"I'm sorry, ma'am, but he can't see you right now. Once he's cleared by the doctor, we'll have to take him into custody."

"What?" she cried. "But it was Garrett. He made him do all of this."

"We'll get it all sorted out. He'll go before the judge today."

"Please, can I see him for just a second? Please," she begged, crushing Ezra's soul.

The officer finally relented, and Charlotte burst through the curtain. "Are you okay?"

Ezra nodded as he opened his arms to her. She fell into them, and even the pain of her body pressing on his was nothing compared to the way his heart soared at the mere feel of her body against his.

She touched his face. "He hurt you." Tears welled in her eyes. "But you're alive. Thank God, you're alive."

Tears fell down his cheek. He wanted to tell her that everything would be okay, but besides the fact that his jaw was bruised, he didn't know if anything would ever be okay again. Instead, he pulled her tighter and held onto her.

"Ma'am, you're going to have to clear the room now. If we can get him to the jail and processed soon, he'll see the judge today."

"You aren't going to put him in with Garrett, are you? He'll kill him."

"No, ma'am. He'll go straight to the medical ward. Now if you'll let us do our job, we need to get him to the jail and process him, otherwise, he won't see the judge until morning."

Charlotte leaned up and kissed his cheek. "I love you, Ezra McCain. I'll be praying for you."

Hearing those words made everything he'd gone through worth it. He pulled her close, then let her go.

"I'll see you at the courthouse," she said and rushed out of the room.

Once processed, they assigned Ezra a public defender where he could plead his defense. Although hiring his own lawyer would've been a much better choice, they advised him that the judge would likely release him on his own recognizance and could then hire his own lawyer.

After telling his story from the time he was ten and met Garrett Malone, the attorney was shocked at all he had experienced.

"I can't tell you what the judge will decide," the public defender said. "But I will request a full investigation into what you're telling me. I am going to request you be released with a court date later in the year. This will give us time to make your case."

28

CHARLOTTE

Charlotte sat in the courthouse next to Cole, listening to each case as it was presented. One by one offenders came before the judge and sentences were given, plea bargains met, or continuations requested.

Finally, a group of men was escorted into the room, all of them wearing orange uniforms and shackles with long chains connecting their wrists to their ankles. She found Ezra among the faces, and her heart dropped. His cheeks were even more bruised than they had been in the hospital. She'd not slept at all since Cole had woken her up. She'd done nothing but prayed the entire time that God would grant Ezra mercy.

Charlotte held her breath as Ezra went before the judge. Cole touched her arm and smiled at her sadly. She was glad he was there to support her. They'd talked extensively and agreed that Ezra deserved a break. He'd been through so much already. But the decision was not up to them, it was up to the judge.

The judge looked through the file on his desk and then up to Ezra. "Looks like you've been through a bit, young man."

Ezra nodded.

"Your lawyer is requesting a continuance on your behalf, and he's informed me that you wish this to go to trial, is that correct?"

"Yes sir," Ezra mumbled through the bandages on his face.

He thumbed through the paperwork again. "I'm going to grant that request because it looks to me like you will need some time to establish your case," he said, then looked to the attorneys who stood back, waiting. "Does the state have any argument with releasing him at this time, pending trial?"

"No, sir. We have found no evidence he is a harm to himself or anyone else."

"You understand that your release today on your own recognizance does not mean you're free of charges?"

"Yes, sir."

"And you agree to be here on the date set by the court for trial?"

"Yes, sir."

"You're hereby released. Please see the secretary for your court date."

Ezra walked to the secretary and a few minutes later, an officer escorted him out of the back court.

"Where's he going?" Charlotte turned to her brother. "I thought they released him."

"I don't know," Cole answered.

"Charlotte Spencer?" a man called, and she stood. It was Ezra's attorney.

"Let's go into the hall," he said.

Once in the corridor, he explained to her it would take another long while for Ezra to be officially released. "I advise you to go home and get some rest. You look tired. Is his vehicle here?"

"Yes." She pulled the key from her purse. "But I want to be here when he's released."

"It could be awhile. He has to go through processing, and I think he might need some time to work this all through. He's requested you not stay."

"What? Why?"

"That's something I can't say, but I think maybe you should give him some time and respect his wishes."

"Okay. I guess." Her heart dropped. She handed over the keys to Ezra's car and left.

Cole followed behind her.

"Just give him time. He's been through a lot. Besides, you need some sleep. We all do."

She walked down the steps of the courthouse. "Where will he go? He has no money. No phone. What if he needs me?"

Cole placed a hand on her back. "He knows where we live. He'll come around when he's ready."

29

———

EZRA

Ezra waited around for five more hours before they released him from jail. His attorney had come by and told him the keys to his car were left with his property, and he would be able to get them upon release.

It saddened him to turn Charlotte away, but he had so much more to think about. He needed to clear his head and do what was right for her. He had no idea what that was, but he wouldn't be able to reason with her there. The attorney had given him many things to think about. He'd been advised to plead not guilty of all charges, and he wasn't sure if that was what he wanted to do. He *was* guilty, and he wanted to own up to it, yet in the same token, he didn't want to waste the rest of his life away in a jail cell.

Once released, he grabbed his belongings and got into his car. There was only one person he wanted to speak to, and he knew right where to find him. He headed for the local fast-food restaurant and made his way to the bridge where he would surely find Stanley, the vet that had given him so much to think about before.

He was greeted happily by the homeless as he handed out burgers to all.

"What happened to you, man?" Stanley asked. "Looks like you got into a nice brawl."

Ezra sat down next to him. With his jaw still in pain, he could only take small nibbles of a burger. "It's been rough."

"So, I see. You wanna talk about it?"

It was the reason he came, so with another bite of his burger, he laid it all out to Stanley. "I'm struggling, man. I want to do what's right, but my lawyer is telling me to plead not guilty. I just want to tell the truth."

"And what is the truth?" Stanley asked. "How you see it?"

"I did a lot of bad things, man. I want to come clean."

"I get that. It makes sense. Have you come clean before God?"

"I have."

"And you don't think God can defend you in a court of law?"

"I'd hire Him, but I think He's probably busy."

Stanley chuckled. "He's got your back, man. Pleading not guilty doesn't mean you're saying you're innocent. It means the state has to prove your guilt. Let them do their job, man. And remember when we talked about that PTSD stuff?"

"Yeah?"

"I don't know the legal term, but man, you've been through some stuff. If you plead guilty, you get no trial. No one hears your story. You just get sentenced. Don't you want someone to hear what you've been through?"

He really didn't. "I don't want people to feel sorry for me, man. I just want—"

"It's not about feeling sorry. You deserve a fair trial. You may not believe it, but that man influenced you as a child. There's no reason for some grand decision to commit the rest of your life to jail. What about that girl? You love her, right?"

"I do. But I want her to accept me as a whole person. One who is free of his transgressions."

"You let the law do that. Don't go setting your own sentence. In the meantime, you go see that girl. Make the best of what time you have. I bet she's worried sick about you."

Ezra wanted to see Charlotte more than anything. He had so

many things to tell her, but everything was so uncertain. He still didn't know what would happen to him in the future. "I just don't want to cause her any more pain. If I go to jail, where will she be in all of it?"

"Let me see here." Stanley put his hand out. "You ever killed anyone?"

"No."

He put out a finger.

"Injured anyone?"

"No."

He put out a second finger.

"Rape, kidnapping, extortion?"

"No! Not even an armed robbery. I've never even shot a gun."

"Well, hows I see it, you ain't looking at much time for some petty theft you done mostly while you was a minor under the influence of an adult who knew better. Don't count yourself noble. You got just cause, and any judge would be ashamed not to recognize it."

The more he thought about it, the more he realized that he'd allowed Garrett's constant scare tactics to create fear within him. He could handle whatever the judge set down for him.

"Okay. Yeah."

"When's your court date?"

"January."

"Good Lordy! You got plenty of time. You go and get yourself settled. Get a job and do well for yourself. The judge will see that you ain't getting yourself into any trouble. He might only order a bit of that kooky counseling to get your mind right."

Ezra chuckled. He was feeling better already. He refused to allow Garrett continue to run his life from behind a jail cell.

"I have some things to do." Ezra stood.

"You gonna go see your girl?" Stanley asked.

"Yep. But I got a couple of stops before that."

Ezra shook hands with Stanley, said goodbye to everyone and promised he would be back.

30

CHARLOTTE

harlotte sat by the fire as the sun went down. Cole sat across from her and Samantha next to him. Cole strummed his guitar while Samantha sang beautifully. The guests roasted marshmallows, hot dogs, and chatted amongst themselves, but Charlotte felt empty. She needed to get her emotions together. The guests were what kept the money coming in, paid the bills, but she just couldn't seem to connect with them.

Cole and Samantha had tried to encourage her, but without Ezra, she was vacant. Why hadn't he wanted to come back? Hadn't she been clear about her love for him? She felt stupid for even saying it. Obviously, it meant nothing to him.

"I'm going to hit the hay," she said, standing. "Stay out here as long as you like." She put on a smile. "I'll see you all in the morning."

Everyone waved and told her goodnight. Cole gave her a worried look, and she smiled back at him sadly. She just couldn't muster the energy to pretend anymore. Robotically, she performed her nightly duties of checking on the horses and locking the store, then went inside the house.

She made herself a hot cup of tea and sat at the table. Feeling as depressed as she had when she'd lost her father and then her mother, she placed her head in her hands and tried to stave off the tears.

A knock at the door startled her, and she almost called out for Cole to get it. But Cole was still out with the guests. Wanting to crawl into her bed and drown in a sea of tears, she stood. The knock came again, and she sighed. Life had to go on for her. So, she went to the door.

As she opened it, Ezra stood on her porch, holding a huge box wrapped in Christmas paper.

"What in the world?" She stared at the box.

"I, uh—" He looked down. "Oh, that. Well, I got you something. And the ladies at my dad's nursing home helped me wrap it. All they had was Christmas wrap."

"Where have you been? I've been so worried about you!"

"Can I come in?" he said, barely opening his bruised jaw. "This is getting heavy."

"Oh. Yeah." Her heart felt lighter with each look at him. "Come on in. What is this?"

"Open it." He sat on the couch and set it down in front of him.

Charlotte sat next to him, and he slid the box in front of her.

"I feel so silly. It's not even my birthday. And certainly not Christmas."

"But it's a special day."

"It is?"

"Open and see."

Charlotte slowly pulled the wrapping paper from the box. The outside contained a picture of a microwave. She raised her eyebrows.

"Just a box I found. Open it up."

Charlotte pulled the massive amounts of tape from the seam and opened the flaps. Her mouth opened in surprise. Inside were several bolts of plush material. There were browns and tans and grays. She pulled one up and put it to her face. "What does this mean? Where did you get the money for this?"

"Keep going." He nodded.

Charlotte set the fabric on the couch beside her and pulled out several packs of buttons and threads in all colors. At the bottom was a small black box. She stared at it unable to move.

"Is that what I think it is?"

Ezra reached down and picked up the box. He opened it, and an engagement ring sat inside, gleaming at her. It wasn't anything glamourous, but it was beautiful to her.

"Ezra, where did you——"

"I'll explain in a minute, but first." Ezra got down on one knee. "Charlotte Renee Spencer, I have loved you from the day I met you. You don't know this, but I spent a good amount of my childhood sneaking to the back window of your stables just to get a peek at you. I know I have done some bad things in my life, and I am prepared to pay for those things. I can't promise life will be great for a while. I might have to … well, we will see what happens. But today, I am putting all of that aside. I'm making a promise before God, and you, that I will be the best man I can be, I will take care of you, love you, and honor you, if you will be my wife."

Tears flooded her eyes. Her hand shook as she held it out. "Yes."

Ezra leaned in and kissed her.

"Now tell me where you got all of this," she demanded half-heartedly.

"I wanted to tell you sooner, but I was afraid you'd think I was trying to buy your love, and then all that happened and well, my father, he left me a good sum of money when he sold his house. He told me to do something good with it, and I plan to do just that."

"What do you mean?"

"It's our money, Charlotte. We can make this ranch what you always dreamed of. And if you will let me, I'll help you get it back to where it's profitable again. You shouldn't have to struggle alone. And if I have to go away, I want to know that you're being taken care of."

"But that's your money. You should spend it on a lawyer. The best one money can buy."

"God will take care of me. Isn't that what you've always told me? For now, let's focus on us. In six months when I go to court, I want to be sure you have everything you need. We'll wait to get married until afterward. I don't want you tied down to me."

Charlotte wiped her tears away. "Whatever happens, I'll wait for you."

EPILOGUE

"Has a verdict been reached?" the judge asked.

"Yes, your honor." A man stood.

"Would the defendant stand."

Ezra stood. His hand still in Charlotte's.

"Please read the verdict to the court."

"We the jury, have found the defendant, Ezra McCain not guilty by reason of coercion on all counts."

"Very well." The judge nodded, and the juror took his seat. "Ezra McCain, I find this decision very agreeable. The life you have led has been a hard one. I commend you for your honesty and ability to overcome these circumstances. I am however ordering you to a minimum of six months counseling."

Ezra thanked the judge and was dismissed. Turning to Charlotte, he lifted her off the ground and kissed her.

"Now can we get married?" she asked. "I've been waiting for ages."

Ezra laughed. "Yes, my love. Now we can get married."

ENJOYED THIS BOOK? YOU CAN MAKE A DIFFERENCE.

Do reviews intimidate you? Don't know exactly what to say? There is no right or wrong. As a reader, you have amazing influential power in helping others decide which books to read. If you enjoyed my words … please take a minute to write a few of your own and let others know.

To leave a review of − *The Cowboy's Forbidden Bride* −click here[1]

Thank you very much!

---

1. https:www.amazon.com/dp/B07PKS1H85

SNEAK PEEK — THE BILLIONAIRE'S UNWELCOME HOME
CHAPTER 1 - MAYA

Maya Brown kneeled down before her five-year-old son, Benjamin, and smiled. "You almost got it right, buddy. Give it one more try. This time, pull a little tighter."

Benjamin slumped his shoulders and tried tying his shoes one more time. "You do it much better, Mommy. Mine always comes undone."

"Practice makes perfect." Maya ruffled his soft, brown curls. "One more time. Mommy's going to be late for work if you don't hurry."

"Will mean Mr. James make you work late again if you're not on time?" Benjamin had never met his grandfather. Mean Mr. James did not know Benjamin's existence. Little Benjamin was Maya's best kept secret.

"Now, Benjamin." Maya tried to reprimand her son, but she could hardly blame him for speaking the truth. "Mr. James is not *always* mean. He did give Mommy a job, right?"

"I guess so." Benjamin pulled his laces tight, but even after all of his effort, they still flopped loosely to the ground. "He should let you come to work whenever you want."

Maya tied her son's shoes for him and then pulled the loops into a double knot. "What kind of world would it be if everyone could just come and go whenever they wanted?"

Benjamin giggled, making Maya wish she could spend the day with him instead of working on a Saturday. But she owed the James family too much to press the issue. "Mrs. James will be here soon. You enjoy spending the day with her, don't you?"

"She's fun, Mommy. But how come I never get to meet Mr. James?"

"You don't want to meet him." Maya lowered her brows and growled like a bear. "He's just an old grump, anyway."

Benjamin giggled as she kissed his nose.

No, she was the one who would have to deal with the ornery man. Better her than Benjamin, though. And Maya would do anything for her son. He was the one and only good thing in her life. If it meant sucking up to rich, white folks so that her son had everything he needed, that was what she would do. Besides, she and Claire James had forged the deal before Benjamin was ever born — Mrs. James would take care of Benjamin's every need and Maya would keep her mouth shut about who his father was. Mr. James would never know he was a grandfather. And Jesse — he would never find out he had a son.

It broke Maya's heart to keep Benjamin away from Jesse, but being that she hadn't seen him since the night they'd conceived, almost six years before, Maya had no other choice. It was what it was, and Maya had no right to put her son through poverty just because she still harbored a crush for his father. If Jesse James had wanted to be with her, he'd have found a way. Maya hadn't gone anywhere. She was still stuck in the same small town of Trust, Arizona, living her life under the rules and restrictions of Jesse's mother.

The doorbell rang.

"Hurry, hurry." Maya rushed Benjamin to the door. "We don't want to keep Mrs. James waiting."

Benjamin grabbed his backpack from the hook by the door and flopped it over his shoulder. He loved his grandmother, even if he didn't know who she was to him. And although Mrs. James adored him too, she refused to divulge the information to anyone that her family's twenty-four karat blood was tainted with African-American blood.

Although his light brown hair was filled with soft curls, his skin was as warm as honey, and his eyes held a tinge of green like his father's, the truth was not to be spoken. From the day he was born, Benjamin had been taken care of, spoiled with whatever he wanted and needed, and would always have the best of everything. He would only miss one small thing — a father.

"Good morning, Master Benjamin." Constance, Mrs. James's personal assistant, smiled at the boy. "Mrs. James is waiting for her favorite little boy in the car. Are we ready?"

Benjamin nodded heartily. Mrs. James would spend the day spoiling Benjamin, while Maya spent it working for Mr. James.

"Good. Come along, then." Constance took Benjamin's hand. "Your car will be here shortly." Constance nodded to Maya. Although Constance was as black as Maya was, Constance looked down on Maya as well. Maybe it was because Maya had stepped over the line by getting involved with a rich, white boy. Constance closed the door behind them, leaving Maya to stare at her surroundings. One night. One stupid night, and Maya's life had changed forever. And the worst part about it was that Maya had known better. Her mother had warned her from the very beginning.

"White people don't understand, Maya. They think, just because slavery has been over for all these years, that there is no racism in the world." Her mother had tried to explain that to her, but Maya had not understood. "And some people just don't like the idea of races mixing."

"Why are we any different? What does it matter? Aren't we all the same on the inside?"

"Please, Maya. You do your job over there and come home. Don't go catching feelings for a boy you can never be good enough for."

But Maya had been young and stupid. She had never known true racism until the day when the entire school found out she was pregnant. Maya had been the product of ridicule ever since.

Although gossip spread about her and Jesse leaving the junior prom together, the rumors were squashed. And then she was labeled with derogatory names she'd rather not repeat. But those names still hurt her to this very day. And then the inevitable happened. Jesse's mother had gotten wind of her pregnancy and the next thing she knew, she was whisked off to some school for pregnant women and hadn't been allowed to come back until after Benjamin was born and she had graduated high school. They had hidden her away and taken care of her ever since.

A few minutes later, another car came to escort her to work. Unlike the limo with driver and all the amenities that came for Benjamin, Maya's car was a taxi. Grabbing her purse, Maya didn't let it get to her on that day any more than it had for the last five years. Reminding herself where she could be, she gave thanks for where she was.

"Good morning, Maya," Hailey said as Maya climbed inside. "Working on Saturday again?"

"I sure am. Looks like you got a hold of the Saturday shift too."

"Yep." Hailey pulled her messy blonde hair into a ponytail behind her head. "Baby needs diapers. Besides, no one tells Claire James no. Not that I work for her, but yeah, well, I guess just about everyone works for her in some capacity."

Maya laughed. She and Hailey had been fast friends from the day they met, and there was no baby that needed diapers.

It was funny how some people didn't pay attention to the color of a person's skin at all, where others, even in this day and age, it was all they could see. Racism went both ways, though. Just as many black people hated the whites. Over a hundred and fifty years had passed since slavery, and still, some people couldn't figure out how to get along.

Hailey pulled the taxi up to the towering James building, where dozens of ambulances and police cars idled outside.

"What's going on?" Maya asked, leaning forward in her seat.

"Looks like someone must have gotten hurt." Hailey placed the car in park. "I hope it wasn't one of those homeless guys who like to sleep on the bench out front. I heard—" She stopped mid-sentence. "Wait! Is that Mr. James?"

Maya scooted on to the edge of her seat and squinted out the window as EMTs pushed a gurney with an overweight, pale, white man strapped to the bed. Maya clasped her hand over her mouth. "That *is* Mr. James!"

"Is he dead?" Hailey's eyes were as big as cannonballs.

"I sure hope not!" She'd never wished a person dead in her entire life. Still, she wondered, would things change if Mr. James were… dead?

"What do we do? Should I just drop you off here?" Hailey looked back at Maya, who was still staring in stunned silence at Mr. James, who was being loaded into an ambulance. "Or do I take you back home?"

"Uh… I don't know."

HAVE YOU READ THESE TITLES?

The Billionaire's London Bride

She's impulsive and outgoing. He's ... not.

Raven Hartly has been through a tremendous life-altering experience. When her best friend invites her on a week-long London vacation, she can't pack her bags fast enough. Set on getting away from reality, her only plan for the trip is to mindlessly enjoy herself.

Shy and reserved billionaire, Emmett Hunt is off to London to appease his older brother who is set on expanding the family business overseas. The idea is absurd, and Emmett would rather be doing anything else. His plan is to get in and get out, then go home and let his brother down easy.

When Raven and Emmett meet, their personalities couldn't be more different yet that only enhances their attraction to each other. But neither of them know how to get over the pain of their pasts.

Trigger Warning: Miscarriage

The Cowboy's Forbidden Bride

After the loss of her parents, Charlotte struggles to keep the family ranch going for her and her younger brother, Cole.

Ezra has a criminal past he'd like to escape, so when his boss pushes him too far, he runs despite the consequences.

When Cole rides up with a dying stranger strapped to the back of his horse, Charlotte recognizes the man she's met only once but never forgot. He doesn't want to put her life in danger, but he's too weak to leave.

She knows she needs to send him away to protect Cole and the ranch, but she'll do anything she can to keep him there...

The Act of Falling

Bekah, a singer at a local Long Beach night club, is a magnet for bad boys. When her boyfriend, Blade, gets arrested, she leaves everything behind, including her beloved guitar, to find something … else. Out of gas but with a plan, Bekah stops in the pristine little town of Sunshine, Arizona.

Ezekiel, the son of the town preacher, is also a teacher at the church's private school. He's quite content in his life and secure in his surroundings. Well, mostly … From the moment Bekah shows up in the church office, wearing a skirt shorter than a man's imagination, a hoop nose ring, and a tattoo of a spider on her back, Ezekiel's quiet little world shifts into territories unknown.

But no worries … she'll be gone by morning.

The Law of Falling

An officer of the law, a social worker, an ornery grandmother, and a flat tire.

When Samantha's grandmother takes a fall in her home, Samantha's parents worry she's not fit to live alone anymore. To her disdain, Samantha seems to have drawn the short straw and now must go out and evaluate her grandmother's situation.

It's only been a short time since Garrett has graduated from the police academy, and being a police officer is nothing like he'd thought. He is sorely missing the kids at the church where he used to teach. But when an attractive woman rolls into town with a flat tire, Garrett is intrigued with the newcomer.

Before they know it, Samantha and Garrett find themselves spending time together, and Gramma Matt may just be the cause of it...

The Billionaire's UnWelcome Home

A car crash reunited them, yet threatened to tear them apart.

After receiving word of his father's illness, Jesse James was hesitant to return home. He'd joined the military to get away from the billionaire and everything he stood for. But when his mother insisted he return, he conceded.

He was in no way prepared for what awaited him...

Monetarily, Maya's life couldn't be more perfect. Working for the James family, her son's every need was taken care of. That was, so long as she kept the family secret. But something was missing, and when Jesse showed up in town, Maya's life became much more complicated...

Love became a complication as Jesse and Maya fought for their right to become a family.

This is an interracial love story with racist themes.

Her Billionaire Dream

He's building an empire. She's cleaning it.

After years of reviving the family business from the ashes his father left, Chandler Jones has no time for a serious relationship. He has no need for companionship and only dates his high school sweetheart because she's equally rich, extremely independent, and looks good on his arm. But when she ducks out on him on the most important weekend of the year, Chandler is desperate.

Dena Gysler wants nothing to do with her rich, arrogant employer. She cleans his office, and he has no idea she exists which suits her just fine. When he offers her ten thousand dollars to accompany him to his weekend business conference, Dena is appalled. But ten thousand dollars is a lot of money for a cleaning lady to refuse.

Dena and Chandler agree to a strictly-business plan that will benefit them both. And falling in love is not a part of that plan.

But then again ... plans change.

To find out more about these characters and their lives check out the rest of the stories in this series.

Her Billionaire Jackpot — Max and Chloe — Mixed-up Marriage

Her Billionaire Wish — Zach and Chelsea — Cruise Ship Romance

Her Billionaire Chauffeur — Boss and Lara — Stranded Together

Her Billionaire Scoundrel — Jax and Jewel — Road Trip

Finding Alissa

When Alissa Martin finds out her fiancé is cheating on her, she's so distraught that she packs a suitcase and leaves. Too upset to think of anything but her fiancé's deception, she ends up in a car accident. Upon awakening in the hospital in the town of Trust, Arizona, she has lost her memory.

Already confused and frustrated, she is shocked when the stranger in her room tells her that she's a loving wife and mother of three.

Even after a year, Derek Andrews mourns the loss of his wife. But his wealthy father-in-law thinks it's time to move on. So much so, that he threatens to cut Derek off if he doesn't find a mother for the children. But could he ever love another woman?

When he comes upon the wreckage of a woman who looks identical to his Elle, he devises a scheme to make her a part of their family...

To find out more about these characters and their lives check out the rest of the stories in this series.

Loving Josie — A Rags to Riches Story

Reclaiming Bailey — A Second Chances Story

Chasing Kennedy — An Online Love Story

To read these and more click on Tayla Alexandra's Author Page to see her full list of books.

GET FREE BOOKS AND EXCLUSIVE TAYLA ALEXANDRA MATERIAL

Connecting with readers is one of the greatest things about writing. I send a weekly newsletter with details on new releases, special offers, and other news tidbits related to my writing.

By signing up for my mailing list, not only will you get exclusive insider news, I'll send you the following titles for free in your choice of Kindle, ePub, or pdf versions

To Trust Again, A Novella

Brother of the Bride, A novelette

Wrapped in Love, A Christmas short

Sign up here[1] for exclusive member access and your free ebooks.

---

1. https://dl.bookfunnel.com/ptrgwt4xc4

ABOUT THE AUTHOR

Tayla Alexandra is the author of Her Sweet Billionaire Romance Series, Finding Trust Romance Series among several others. She makes her online home at Tayla Alexandra Books. You can connect with Tayla on Twitter, on Facebook , and you can send an email at TAlexandraAuthor@gmail.com

facebook.com/talexandraromance

twitter.com/AlexandraTayla

amazon.com/author/taylaalexandra

bookbub.com/profile/tayla-alexandra